THE RED BIRD

*Also by John Fraser
and published by
AESOP Modern Fiction:*

Animal Tales
Black Masks
Blue Light / Starting Over
The Case
Down from the Stars
Enterprising Women
Hard Places
An Illusion of Sun
The Magnificent Wurlitzer
Medusa
Military Roads
The Observatory
The Other Shore
The Red Tank
Runners
Soft Landing
The Storm
Three Beauties
Wayfaring

THE RED BIRD

John Fraser

AESOP Modern Fiction
Oxford

AESOP Modern Fiction
An imprint of AESOP Publications

Martin Noble Editorial / AESOP
28 Abberbury Road, Oxford OX4 4ES, UK
www.aesopbooks.com

First paperback edition published by AESOP Publications
Copyright (c) 2015 John Fraser
First hardback edition published by AESOP Publications
Copyright (c) 2016 John Fraser

www.johnfraserfiction.com

ISBN: 978-1-910301-24-1

Contents

Empty Rooms

Hugo writes: 'I keep a red bird in a cage. I don't approve, of course, but he's like us, outside the cage he'd not survive. He's a bright little guy – like my superego, my intelligence, he stands there most of the day, watching me. Not contributing, of course. If you visit, he'll surely take you in ... see his black stony eye!

'I've tried my hand at earth moving – no, not orgasms as a gigolò, but driving a heavy beast, with a huge horn on its nose. A machine.

'As for your disbelief – treasure it, and all the secret truths it holds. The guys here – they've never been a nation. We thought that they should be one, at least trying, like the rest. For the others, we made the threat – to arms, citizens! The threat sufficed. Then, to toughen them all – a stretch of capitalism. Calm the whites all over. "Excuse me!" everybody says. No one wants their servants getting uppity, buying machetes in the market. Instead, a show of striving, and docility. Then maybe we'd see. Some gentle socialism. Everyone – all up for it.

'You are right, of course. The socialism that should have been the goal – that's all gone dead. We've dug out all the wealth. The guys are poor, and ignorant. Those phases that we thought we'd engineer – they haven't sequenced. Everything is stuck. No revolution.

'Keep your truth close to yourself. It's quite irrelevant.

'Once a day, the red bird climbs on the highest stick, and sings his whole song, the trills, the melody, the hero's call, the triumph, and the *dies irae*. Come and listen to him. I don't have much room, but for a night, you can make do. Hear the bird through twice at least – maybe he'll change his tune for you.'

There's a note on the back: 'Don't ask the cops where my place is. Our armed wing didn't fight much, but it thinned out our dissent. All the big bosses now were survivors of their purges. Intruders scare them, and they defend themselves against the ghosts.' He scrawls on, 'There was this sweet old man. He'd do anything, so's not to go to jail again. He was set up to be friends – with everyone. They all drank it in, like it was love potions.'

I don't go, of course. There's interesting things around, without seeking out the dangerous ones.

I tell Marcel, 'Hugo's got quite reactionary.' He doesn't believe me. Maybe he doesn't understand the word.

'Shall you go?' asks Marcel. 'Hugo is sour, of course. There's always guys who think they have decided everything, and then it turns out otherwise.'

'It's not safe there,' I tell Marcel. 'Of course I shan't be going. Hugo's lost the pleasure of observing paradox. Contradiction. He used to be a naturalist – then he lost patience. Things slip away so fast, however much you're devoted. Animals quicker still. He eats bush meat now.'

I buy a red bird, though. The guy says, 'He may not sing. He's young.'

He doesn't sing. Maybe no one taught him to.

I think of Hugo as a precursor. Africa – as a biblical land: enslavement, tribes, kings, prophets and idols. Backsliding and plagues. Expulsions and exodus. Wraths of God. Those old radicals, gone into their wilderness. Hugo, bored among his animals, scientifically observing creatures quite unscientific. Now down to his caged bird. Everyone waiting for the wealth, and meanwhile digging it up and shipping it out. I tell Marcel,

'Hugo's out of cash. He's doing heavy work. It makes his point.'

'He's got a few more years,' says Marcel. 'I for sure can't sub him.'

'They nicked his car and phone,' I say. 'That's why he writes. He's satisfied, he said – they did what they had to, making transition clean and swift. They can't stop the new guys stealing and running brothels.'

'He loved a lot of people,' Marcel says. 'Black and white, and nothing in between. That's what he said. It wasn't true. Sometimes, he loved everyone. Other times, he was more a realist.'

'The air there is special pure,' I say. 'There was an observatory – the old kind, hole in the roof, and sextant on the floor. They heard the final messages from stars, as they went ploff!'

'People don't live on stars,' Marcel says. 'They live on rocks that circle round.'

'Those messages, the final words...' I say.

'I'm sure ours have been written. Who by, I'd like to know. Some guy we didn't tell him to, I bet,' he says, and pulls a face. 'Terrible. The human age – summed up in seven words.'

'Hugo told me he hears the last accounts in Xhosa, drifting off the stars. That must be the language of the universe. That's as it all should be,' I say. 'Though guys on the stars – they maybe don't look like us at all.'

'Why shouldn't other people look like us?' asks Marcel, squaring up.

'Well,' I say, 'the shape is clumsy. Then there's clothes, on, off. And farts. The design is fairly crap.'

'I've heard,' says Marcel, cooling down. 'Those messages gave Hugo a revealing key. All the big books – are really marginalia. Who would imagine gods would write some stuff that left creation sceptical? Hugo has sketched the real book, the ur, the book of books. "Capital" was just a footnote. The bible – just the lyrics and some lists of relatives, to go with a far greater work, a brick of wisdom and foretells.'

'I'm not convinced,' I say. 'Besides – those women, Hugo's. Not everyone was sure it was a good idea....'

'Going with women,' Marcel says, 'it's like the races, or the gaming wheel. You do it for the rush, the kick – but in the end to lose, be punished. And to start again, or not.'

'Hallucinations, thoughts, dreams...' I say. 'Hugo's forever a materialist. Those are the clues. They all come from the grey sponge he wears behind his eyes. But – who is to judge, the right, the wrong? And that big text, elusive...in his fantasy, perhaps?'

'Of course we judge,' Marcel says. 'Each with what works for where he lives. Hugo was disappointed it ended bad for him. But – disappointment everywhere – it has its cures, its pretexts... Take all those women – you can't conclude with all of them, layered in the bed. Even if you had them all, none of them remains, nor you with them. And so – don't judge, and don't regret. After a while, you see – refinement's painful, but it's best.'

'Hugo wasn't one for cutting out, or cutting down,' I say. 'He wanted narrative, not messages pinned up on a board. Nor farewells – they weren't the text. They were just the key that said – there is a tale, not spoken by a faltering voice, but made of signs engraved. The tale that never ends. Not falling stars – he wanted a story, coherent, upright, on its own.'

'Ah,' Marcel jumps on this. 'But what would that all mean? What's it all about?'

I improvise. 'Well, I think it would be about itself. It would be the string, remaining when all the stars are dead, the string that tied them all, and has no light.'

The red bird hops, buzzes its wings.

'There!' says Marcel, 'it's hungry. Don't you give it water?'

'Of course,' I say. 'I give it everything it wants. It's very moderate. I don't think it would sing, even if it starved. I shan't try, of course.'

We're concerned, about everything. 'Maybe we should take a trip,' I say. 'See Hugo.'

'Tania and I, we could go,' Marcel says.

I thought Tania was my girl.

'Oh, I wouldn't go with you,' says Tania, squinting at me. 'You've got the butterflies, behind your eyes, like your mad friend, Hugo. I'd go with Marcel here,' and she holds his arm.

'You'd inflate it all,' I say. 'The blacks and whites of it.' I guess that's not good taste. I hope they don't set off.

'Oh,' says Tania, 'we know it all already. The world. Everyone knows everything. Dug up, cut up, thought up. All talents on a disc. All the past is present. If the future doesn't come – look! – it is already here. The poet said, "The half is greater than the whole." That is our commonplace, but he had thought that up ten thousand years ago. Half portions, now, for everyone.'

'Well, Tania,' says Marcel, 'if everything is known, all you need do is master it, and everyone.'

'I ought to side with humans, in the last resort,' says Hugo, writing again, 'but I don't. I ought then to side with the animals. But they prey on one another too. I can't shift it on to Nature. Nature's like History. It's a hedge to hide behind, I've planted some myself.'

'There,' says Tania. 'I told you. If you've become a loner, you don't want people visiting.'

We sit in line, we three. We sort of watch TV. The screen is white, then there come wolves. I want to cry, just like they wanted me... Their humanity, their love, the cubs...

'It's made by Disney,' Marcel says. 'So when they shoot the wolves, it's something we don't see.'

'Should I like that?' Tania asks. 'Live in a tent, eat mice, and empathise? Is that what Hugo did?'

'People look happy when they should be suffering,' I say. 'And when the filming stops, maybe the story starts.' Another movie now –

The cops are shooting miners. That's a channel near where Hugo lives.

'I'd work out in America,' Marcel says. 'A personal success. Even here, New York. Except – they're beaten on the battlefield, and now they burn the stuff that ends the world. Sore losers: that I can't abide. It's why I don't play cards.'

'We don't have skills,' says Tania, 'us immigrants. We just grimace. That gets you fired.'

'I can't help anything,' I say. 'This here is not a bird of wisdom, it's a bird of song.'

'You make even mute things seem strange,' says Tina. 'The rest of us is on this raft. Is there land? And are there savages? Do we eat each other? Do we sink? There's answers for each eventuality...'

'I hope he sings,' I say. 'Though I'd not know if it's tradition, or what he's just invented.'

'Just checking,' Marcel says. 'We talk about Hugo, and do nothing more. He said, "We brought the new men. If it's revolution – with the new men comes the Terror. We have the new men, the terror's yet to come. Then – there must be an idea, down in the depths – the giant squid, who turns the ocean black. Even the Reformation was a revolution, Holy Wars. New men, the terror, holy war – and the idea. Sometimes, the new men are just beasts. Sometimes the terror's all you see. If you survive – it is the ink, suffusing all. The squid. Down here – there is no squid. I'm terrified."'

We are silent, digesting that.

'I thought we'd go, cheer Hugo up,' Marcel says. 'Just a human thing. Maybe he's past it, though.'

'These old guys – they make me sad,' says Tania, pleased the trip is off.

'There's only one dark wood,' I say. 'Just one, for everyone. There's birds, and monkeys. Colours you don't see outside. If there is somewhere else, of course, other outsides.'

'Well,' says Marcel, 'there's your psychology. You want out. Somewhere quite colourless, where danger's absent...' He and Tania move away, talking about me.

'He's typical of the sceptic whose persistent dream – the dying dream – is of enthusiasm reborn, finding apotheosis,' Marcel says.

'He was my "older man",' says Tania, 'but he went on getting older.'

'Not as old as Hugo,' Marcel says, pulling her close: 'Hugo collected the money. Maybe he wanted in the end to sign the banknotes. But, of course, he fingered guys. A courtmartial, then they disappeared.'

I interrupt. 'I have to start from my own self, the horror that there is inside. I starts where Hugo ends. Where else? It isn't self-absorption – it's the only way to reach the calm outside: the abstract, the horror quite impersonal, embodying everybody else's. It's the sea of commonality, of common understanding, sharing the dread. It's acceptance, indifference. Life's like that, not like anything else. Then, there's Hugo – trying to change, to live with, the evil: the necessary doing wrong to reach the good that makes a mock of good.'

They stare. Marcel asks, 'Do you roil like this, each time there's maybe need to make a trip?'

To lighten up, I stare at the red bird. He stares back, the unanswered question in his eye. Much interested, on the verge of some reaction – any reaction, if I give a clue. Sing! I have no gesture that conveys. He does communicate, though; perhaps he thinks that's all that's needed. Or can do no more.

Later, I say to Tania, 'I thought we two had something... now, for you it's Africa with Marcel.'

She winds her hand round, as if time was a clock, brim full of seconds: 'It's voyaging,' she says, 'not sticking. You want everything stuck firm in its place.'

'If it isn't in its place, where is it?' I ask.

'Do you like it?' she asks. 'My hair. I had it bobbed.'

'That's just in novels, a century ago,' I say.

'I guess it's in the movie now,' she says. 'You stay quiet here, and fuss about your bird. If it won't sing, teach it to speak.'

'It won't know anything to say,' I say.

Marcel and Tania take a trip, not to Hugo. They don't say where.

Tania sends a card – Extreme Sports, is the land it's from. 'Marcel jumps from aeroplanes. He wants to be wonderful, so it's higher and higher. I run to him, when he lands. I'll tell you when the highest heaven's reached!'

It's the only extreme thing about Marcel. Stepping into nothing – it seems easy, though it's hard enough you wouldn't do it.

Hugo writes, 'Everyone's apologising. What if you don't, if things seemed set, OK a certain way? We were sorry about it then, the killing. Why say we're sorry now?' His card has a scene of gnus running, not aeroplanes stretching for the heights.

When Marcel returns, he's taller. He must have landed well.

'He's still afraid of elevators,' Tania says.

'You can't see where they'll finish up,' says Marcel.

'Quiet,' says Tania loudly. 'We've finished with this crap – the fear, regrets – the doubt. Marcel looks for cures, the rest of you – expect the miracles: the song... Me – I'm quite indifferent.'

'Oh no,' I say, 'I've quite abandoned that, the singing, the instruction. The bird'll live out his life in quiet.'

'Your life,' Tania says to me, 'will be much less than the one you want. Marcel's – beyond his dreams, beyond his imagination.'

'Who cares?' I say. 'What about Hugo?'

'He's part of what happens. Do you think he might have stood aside? Devoted himself to animals? If he's disappointed, so what? As for me – I'm one of those he helped to free, and now – I must think of casting off these chains,' and she holds out wrists, as if she wants assistance, or to assist.

'All kinds of people trained there, like us,' she says. 'Jumping, falling. Gliding, like those spooky planes that bomb, on purple wings. All kinds – hitmen, crusaders. All were there, in sportsland. We aren't at all the bourgeois you might think.'

'I didn't think,' I say. 'Not that it's relevant.'

Tania presses on. 'Follow your sympathies. Start a war. Put the fractured in a camp. Make a nation, sell weapons, pills; sell your brain cells. Sell yourself and renounce the cash. Take your job...'

'It's the new generation, Tania,' I say. 'You wouldn't understand. They move you round from job to job. Some, so's they know what's being done, others so's they don't. It's more contemporary than you, than your "holidays with hoods", your "Spies and warriors" – train together, beat their fears, down from the skies like scalding rain. Knowing where your enemy is dropping. Just muscle and gravity.'

'Marcel follows the trend,' she says, 'then backflips. In the end – he's nothing. I'm something. In the end.'

We contemplate each other's chances, and our hopes.

'Take a flight,' says Tania. 'Leave the bird. They don't let it on the plane, even if it's in your pocket. They fear it has some secret song, that makes you step outside, and fly and glide.'

'Forget the goddam bird,' I say. 'It hops. It isn't made to fly. No whimsy, Tania.'

'Forget yourself!' she says. 'Forget understanding. Just think! – everything that is, was made for you, and only you. And when you die, it disappears, every last star and string, all pasts, all futures. It is only you, and whatever you choose to call an other. It's all yours, your enchantment, your wood, your path. True, you can't choose. Not anything, not even clothes. And – it's injustice, thickly spread for everyone. But – the scene is yours...'

She talks on: 'Tania,' I say. 'That's a crap idea. And not even yours. "No nature, all is art." You'll broadcast it, somehow, and make it true.'

'I know,' she says, 'I've had enough of catching Marcel as he falls from heaven.'

'Marcel hears music as he falls,' I say, 'but doesn't know the notation, so it's lost, unwritten.'

'That's the trouble with guys like you,' Tania says. 'Marcel – he can be heartbreaking, if you care to stand around and wait. But you – you could be anything: a painter, a Croesus of the retail. A Sufi. Getting better: even, if you go to Hugo – black. But somehow – you lack the equipment for any of these. It's a tragedy, but that's a splendour too, when it's performed well.'

'That bird, Tania,' I ask. 'Is it art or nature?'

'Oh,' she says wildly. 'Just bad art, I think. Duration. You must have that as well, or you'd not notice anything.'

'Hugo said duration counted lots,' I say.

'That's not in this argument,' she says, and dismisses me and Hugo.

Tania makes me love the bird more, and hope he doesn't need reciprocate. His eye is always bright, curious. He's interested in the small everything around.

I shan't go to Hugo, nor strive to be what Tania said – a black. What good would that do?

Maybe I'll come back to her.

*

'A miracle!' shouts Marcel. 'A carnage. Oh, the humanity! In pulp. Ketchup and burnt toast!'

'He jumped,' says Tania. 'Then, the plane went down. Marcel's rather garbage, don't you think?'

'That's why we're here,' I say. 'All of us. We jumped in time. But – one shouldn't celebrate. Try to take some guilt.'

'Loud survivors,' Tania says, disgusted. 'The worst sort.'

Marcel lies back in his rocker: 'Our civilisation,' he proclaims, 'is founded on the contradiction – faith, and humanism. I had both, one bore me up, the other wafted me down. The other guys, with only one or other – down they went. Nature had dropped a stitch.'

'Quite insufferable,' Tania says, in general. 'Bad nature.'

'Don't be a prig, Tania,' Marcel says. 'I've an artist interested in my story. Floating down – an angel, or an athlete. No dismal decline. Down bang from the towers, the oft-climbed mountains...The fall, slabbed in plastic, mounted on sticks, like kiddies' windmills. Enacted, musicked, sung in monotone....'

'Angels and athletes!' says Tania, irritated. 'What message have they left to bring?'

'Oh,' says Marcel, rocking, 'the feel of thin air around your thighs.'

'That's all there is to it, then?' asks Tania sternly. 'Bodies without wings, wings without bodies? If you've that presentiment, that we're a species in decline – then you should feel more urgency. Throw some blame.'

'It isn't that,' I say. 'It's looking for some way it all unravels faster. And – nearer what I want.'

'Ah yes,' she says. 'That's more the theme! Breaking from the bridgehead. Stealing a march. Cutting things short, then shorter still.'

'I'm with you, to a point,' says Marcel. 'All the rest – the sequences, the plans, the schemes – they lead to cowards, bullies, and the fear. Speed. That's the thing – hurry it up. Then jump.'

'Marcel,' I say, 'to get you up so high that you can jump – you need a troop of guys. You go down slow alone – they take you up as quick as quick. It's them, they are the trunk, not you. You are their leaf.'

'You guys forget,' says Tania, 'that Hugo's there – a sitting duck. He wanted to go fast – he got things wrong. It's what we must avoid.'

'There was a moment Marcel missed,' I say. 'Before you hit the ground, a shape is formed. Of course, you don't have time to pass it on, describe – it's what the kaleidoscope performs, a symmetry made and multiplied of other symmetries obscure. Marcel didn't hit, the other guys have hit and gone. Hugo takes off, his final gyre, there! look, he's a span above where he will land and hit and understand, and never pass it on.'

'This stuff,' says Tania, 'this fantasy, is what they used to mystify us all. The flying – you can do it backwards, with a pint or two of Stolichnaya, and you hit for sure, and after, everything's the same, though you feel worse.'

This big city – central towers, the teeth still standing proud, all round is rusty gums. Tania and I, entering a listless scene – from difficult places. Marcel has always lived here, doesn't notice anything. We're ready for a move. Marcel has only his story, his feet, his ground, his luck.

Tania says, 'That bird has done the rounds – he travels, he's a nose, an overcoat. His silence is an open ticket. They all get tired of him, and on he moves – a red flag.'

How we talk! I guess it's to keep quiet about the sex, the gyroscope inside that holds us all together.

'Sex?' asks Tania. 'It's not like politics, it happens, and it's done. Or, thinking of you guys – it doesn't happen, and it's never done.' She laughs – Marcel and I, not on her menu.

Hugo blobs up on Tania's screen – first, ectoplasm, then foetal: his mouth closes before the words come out. 'I borrowed this device to show I still exist,' he says. 'It seemed to me that time was just a chain, and history was hitched to it – like an unfinished auto moving regular, expectant, down the line. And it seemed – you could break the chain, or speed it up or slow it down, like many seem to do – or say they have. But now – I think it moves along, inexorable. Maybe in space it's different, it turns a corner. Not for us. You're born to suffer what you must, until your corpse rolls off the end, and some guy drives it off. It's better not to think of better or of worse. Just check that all's in place...' The sound goes off, the baggy face remains, the mouth gurns round the silent thoughts.

'There!' says Tania. 'We've seen Hugo, and his ghostly double too. What a pain he must have been – a demon aspiring to run paradise. Marcel shows – trust to fortune – there is nothing stronger.'

'But no paradise,' says Marcel, 'not even the good place. Just us. Paradise, suffering... that's not it. Everything's connected, nothing coheres. It's all procedures, policies, a heap of carrots, sticks, that bosses

use. Fortune. My luck – that's the only thing that doesn't
fit.'

'Not luck, Marcel,' says Tania. 'Chance. It fits.'

'It's not eternal return that we seem stuck in,' I tell
Tania, as Hugo's face gives a last wriggle, a sperm, its
lighted tail expiring, the screen dark. 'It seems we're
stuck. The rhythm and the key slouch on... We're in
eternal pause.'

'Oh no,' she says to me. 'The dialogue – surely you
can hear – it always changes. And there are people, those
good places too – though why, now Marcel's happy with
his angels, I should waste my time for you – I cannot
think!'

*

She takes me to this tower. 'No,' says Egon, who's alone,
and wears little scythes of beard and sideburns. 'Don't
keep looking out the window. It hasn't happened yet, the
catastrophe. As for its form... we'll have to think again,
about what a landscape is. Anyway, you may never see
the event.'

Tania and I wander about the space – there's nothing
to see, except electric fittings. 'And put your cage down,'
Egon says.

'What's your angle?' I ask. It seems right. The only
angles here are right ones.

'It's survival,' Egon says. 'Not the banal stuff about
leaving marks. Or futurology, the guessing. That guy said
survival was about the more intense form of living. Well,
we're not into that. It's what kind of person we should be,
when we survive. You know that you'll survive the end,
but how? What's your "so what"?'

'It sounds quite precious,' I say.

'Well, I sure hope so,' Egon says. 'We don't want to make a club of it.'

He kisses Tania: 'My! your hair!' he says. 'Pink as candy floss. Those were the days. On the beach. Building castles. Knocking them down. See,' he turns to me, 'after the event, some colours will be missing. Klimt will be monochrome. It'll be all Schiele. Fewer types of grass. No dialectics of nature. Cut to the bone, no counter-cultures. Just one. Culture: if there's enough of us.'

'You mean, it's a hypothesis?' I ask. 'What kinds of people for what kind of world – that we don't know what has happened to it?'

'Yes,' says Egon. 'That's about it. We have seminars, of course. It's not a class thing, though. Intelligence too is not a given.'

'Put so,' says Tania, 'it sounds like everyday uncertainty. But what's different – is the catastrophe. Otherwise – you'd just see neo-goths.'

'Post-goths,' says Egon quietly. 'Think of those Nubians – lost their river to electricity. Us – we're global, we can smite anywhere, so we'd be without everything.'

'We'd lose everything,' Tania agrees. 'But some loss might be a gain.'

Egon looks out the window – it seems he allows himself. I ask Tania, 'What's this guy, Egon, discovered?'

'Oh,' she says, 'we were young lovers. So young, we exchanged families. The swap suited everyone. We climbed buildings together, and jumped down, on roofs. Everyone then was taken with it, a triumph. After, it became a sport. We wanted more. Marcel, though, he's satisfied with very little – his epiphany's enough.'

'Egon,' I say. 'I'm sure you're on the right track. You need a philosophy of the shock. But so far – yes, you have the void. The thinking of the fall; not yet the looking down into the nothing, counting the holes you'll have to dig, cities to bury, species to cancel out – all that. It's the fall, though, the slipping through the nothingness, the cries of – what? Birds? The angels, black and white, squabbling to hold you up or cast you down? And which is which – return to the old, the relatively good? Or to the abyss, which is, perhaps, quite other?'

'Yes,' says Egon gloomily. 'The bird of wisdom, if it flies at all, flies in the dark. You maybe feel its claws, but you don't see its beak. Trains hoot – this bird does not. Its head can swivel – back, forward, to the side – quite unpredictable, and wobbling. The flight's the same: it's flighty...'

Tania interrupts and tells me, 'That woman, Clara, called. The one who says, "I'm Spanish, I'm not a Hispanic." She wants to meet you in the pub, the Empty Room.'

I meet Clara there – we kiss. I kiss her on the mouth. She might be my 'older woman'. She says, 'My son's out for a slash, but he'll be back.' We've nothing more to say, it seems.

'My vagina,' Clara says, 'is full of tiny shell-less snails. We swam together – this river, in Ethiopia, they came aboard. I'd better warn you. Sitting here, I squirm.'

'Of course you would,' I say. 'At school, they told us all about it.'

'Well,' Clara says, impressed, 'they had the prescience, then, that you would go to Africa.'

'Oh no,' I say, 'not a travel lesson, no, quite another sort.' There's silence, as she writhes.

'The people that I know,' I say, 'they all seem middle class.'

'No, upper middle,' Clara says. 'That's the class of choice, of aspiration. Most in the world are destined to disappointment.'

We stare. Her son does not come back. She says, 'Hugo is dying. That's what all these old lefties do. There's nothing left for them, no space, no time. He's disappointed too, but not about his class. Life is more complex now. We all have bigger brains, the Chinese have the biggest ones in town,' she laughs. 'You should go see Hugo,' and I know I won't. I say:

'I saw him when he passed through here. He wanted a safe house. Mine wasn't safe, or anything. I was impressed, and young. He said, "How do you live here, without animals?" I couldn't answer him.'

'It's all politics and science, for Hugo,' Clara says. 'Species collapse now in a blink. Back then, those dinosaurs were around for years. Some beasts are cute, they're saved. The ugly ones – they disappear. That's what Hugo saw. It's all guys who choose to speed things up, or slow them down. "Us animals," he said, "we can decide what, how, and how quick. If we live on in trees, in zoos, in shacks." Here, we're in zoos. Where he is – it's shacks. Trees keep you out the flood. It's true. He's a great man. Except – it didn't go the way he hoped. It got slowed down. Maybe everywhere.'

'Where's your son, Clara?' I ask.

'Oh, he's gone off. He won't come back. He's old enough. They all do that – they often send a card.'

'Once, they'd say he went off to be free,' I say. 'No one talks of freedom any more. Hugo was a great liberator, he wanted to go further than he could, and now

– no one knows what being free might mean. It's all security and cash and power. And the catastrophe, the fear.'

'Yes,' says Clara, '"Free". It has a funny antique sound. A threat. Like kids. "My feeling free means you can't know what it means." Or else "mine's bought, maintained, at the expense of yours".'

'Well,' I say, 'fashions – they change. Poor Hugo.'

'I always thought your friend Tania was superficial,' Clara says. 'But that was nothing, compared to you.'

'We could get drunk,' I say. 'To celebrate your son, his passage to independence.'

'Oh,' she says. 'I'm quite drunk already. But I'm just a tourist here.'

'How can you be a tourist?' I ask. 'Knowing the stories, the presents and the pasts? How it all got fixed, glued together, in that way? Can you just look at landscapes? You go seeking, but what if it happens to you? Being snared, where you're visiting?'

'I'm like Marcel,' she says. 'Once you have fallen, you are charmed. Nothing more can happen to you.'

'It's true,' I say. 'It's these long expositions, being in transition, one lot are into waltz time, the rest are marching on... that's what drags.'

We drink. Some guy has brought some homebrew in a tub.

'That bird of yours,' says Clara. 'I saw flocks of them, quite like. They sing, it's Mahler, and their colour is the red of fires beneath the Rift. One day, all those plates will clash like cymbals, all the buildings will fall down, and we shall face each other, naked, raising our palms and waiting for the word...'

'Where's my bird?' I shout. 'Surely I didn't leave it in that other empty room, where Egon's making out with Tania?'

I can't remember where I left him. In the men's room, where the door says 'Blanks', I find his flattened cage, his home. Oh no, I think, there's that old wounded Clara, crawling on the floor, and I must find the red bird, not waste time to pick her up...

'He hardly sings at all,' says Clara. There! she's holding him. His yellow eye turns to me, and then goes black. I stash him in my pocket. There – he's safe, and silent.

There's a space.

I must have moved in space and time.

I'm safe and silent, on my home floor. Where's Clara? I hurry back to the Empty Room. A song thumps in my head – 'Living in a Dive on Vine'. I call Tania.

The barman says, 'There's no one here. They all find a home, all leave.'

'This is a hole,' Tania says, later. 'They all sell themselves, somehow. In the morning, there's never anyone. Clara's still on tour, somewhere, I feel sure. She hunts, like her son. She'll be following some track.'

'You've no idea where, Tania?' I say.

'If she could walk, someone would have taken her off,' says Tania. 'You thought that was on her mind.'

'She had the *mal d'Afrique*,' I say. 'Not just frivolity, like me. Or you.'

'It's true – just watching things go down, and waiting to adjust to what comes next – it isn't noble,' Tania says. 'Clara's been taken off, for sure. That's tough for her. What more can we do? We each have a disaster, a special one. No one of them is better than the next.'

Would someone buy her, Clara? I wonder.

'We all come from Europe, one way or another,' Tania says. 'At least, we all have European names. When you leave a place as big as a continent, you must be leaving it in ruins.'

'They wouldn't like to hear that, Tania,' I say.

'Oh,' she says. 'They're used to ruins. It's home to them.'

'Here in America,' I say. 'It's quite ruined too,' and we turn towards the window, and don't look out.

'They don't notice here,' Tania says. 'And us – we've nothing to ask of each other. You and I.'

'You're fine with Marcel,' I say.

'Mister Freefall? Yes, he's excellent,' she says.

'Our minds have no peace,' I say. 'They're two cats fighting in a pillowcase.'

'Who wants peace,' she says, 'and it's late for being pretentious. You have it bad, you've mal d'Hugo. Seeing him won't do you any good.'

'I mean minds in general,' I say. 'Not yours and mine.'

'You're not trying to flirt?' she asks. 'That would be a joke. We're laughing all the time. It's like Marcel says, this is funny town. "They sell arms to guys, and then they fight them. They back some guy, he's dumped, and then they fight him. Some guy they've backed gets mad at being dumped, and bombs them back – and they're amazed, offended. They have a new Jerusalem, the others can't have a Caliphate. Compared to this, parachuting is just droll."'

'Marcel'll have us thrown out of America,' I say, 'Talking like that. And then I bet they'll lionise him for it.'

'It's all talk,' says Tania, 'and besides – it's what everybody knows. It's bound to finish bad.'

'Maybe Marcel thinks he has a special angle,' I say, 'you know, "*J'ai seul la clef de cette parade sauvage*".'

'Maybe I should go back somewhere,' Tania says.

'Let's have some drinks,' I say. 'That way we'll focus onto Clara.'

'I'm going to the museum,' Tania says, leaving me. 'There's landscapes, and plaster masks. And colours! You only see them in studios, then they're dug up, shipped here, and framed.'

'Surely you see landscapes with Marcel?' I ask.

'He wears goggles, and I only see up his pantlegs as he descends,' she says. 'I haven't invented landscape yet, it's just expanse, and objects placed around. I try to see things new, as if I'm history first time round.'

Going on like this, we'll all be destitute.

'It's more fun than what you'd otherwise do and be paid for,' I say, 'but it's ridiculous.'

'Well,' she shouts, 'not as much as losing Clara. And Hugo. And not knowing where to look.'

'That's so,' I say. 'And I nearly lost the bird.'

'It makes no sense, your bird. A thing, that's a problem, too,' she says. Then, 'This scene here is crap,' she says. 'The shame of it, it hurts your blood. And yet, it's the best place you'll ever know.'

*

A guy, what they once called 'coloured', comes from Egon's place. I laugh, thinking of Tania, her seeking colours, colouring herself. 'No, I don't drink,' the guy says. Then, 'We're doing as well as we can expect... as badly, too.'

'I know Hugo sent you, to say to visit him,' I say.

'Oh no,' the guy says, 'he doesn't give orders any more. I'm not here for him – I'm here to see some guys. We sell crowd control, you know. Sticks, shields, and gas.'

'Hugo was my hero, when he passed through,' I say, looking back, 'He was those things you'd choose to die for.'

'He's dying now,' the guy says. 'Willingly or not. You might arrive too late, and that's a waste.'

'It might make no difference,' I say. 'I don't do anything much for very long. It's like the others here, the citizens, the butterflies.'

I don't trust the guy.

He says, 'Those Tuaregs – they live in hell. The paradise that they call Azawad – is also hot as hell. No wonder God seems their last chance. You could go visit them. If you've no friends, no cash, you'll not be kidnapped, you might say farewell before they disappear. Collect the music, tape the voices. I flew over.'

It is my scene, but I shan't go.

He goes off, to make his pitch.

'Tuaregs? You?' says Tania.

'Tuaregs, us?' I say. 'We already feel like them, we trail across the hot sand...'

'Maybe, if Clara called me...' Tania says. 'She'd have the modern skills you need. We wouldn't fight or trade, of course... She knows her way.'

'There's lots of sickness, I believe,' I say.

'And fighting too. I might need... my military training,' Tania says.

'It's not like that. It's random. Besides, you'd never have decided to train,' I say. 'Service, armies...'

'How do you know?' she asks. 'I might have had to do it, then decided to change sides.'

'It's not a choice, Tania,' I say, though I've no idea.

'Those people have come to the end, it seems,' Tania says. 'That's when you can start to dream. That's what Egon says. To me, it sounds like crap. They're thinking hard, it's not a dream. We should go down, watch them. But – we need some company. Clara won't call me. Beneath it all, she is quite sensitive. Must we find someone to come with us? Egon? He always says the same. It's like the rhythm of the camels, getting into the music. He only knows the one song. It's not the sort you can join in.'

'Tania? No, no, I can't see her,' Clara said. 'I'm in black and white, a charcoal stick, and she's a chromo.'

Egon was a soldier, from a family of them, like they came out of a box. He steps out from his line of catastrophes.

Marcel set out to win him – tempting a fall by falling – seeking to impress, forever stepping out on gravity.

Hugo, and the 'crimes of the Stalin era'. Shall we ever forget those? Of course, most people have, not Hugo.

We three – me, Egon, Marcel, – the three graceless – sit in the Empty Room. There's a space where you can express yourself, or anything. Try singing, suicide, or telling jokes. Tania is there, dancing before us. She wears a woollen skin, dark green, she slithers on the dark moquette, she spins, turns arms into legs, makes her head fade out – forward, and back. It is a marvel. What does it signify, apart from practice, anguish? She is in tears. The space is there for that as well.

She stops. 'There,' she says. 'Do you care more for each other now? Is there understanding?'

'You've a talent, Tania,' Egon says, 'but that we knew. Our feelings – are our own. Sharing them diminishes.'

Tania says to me, 'You were so good. You travelled. That's what you can do, must do again.'

She wants to humanise us more.

'I bring nothing back,' I say. 'The philosophies fall under the wheels of the train.'

'Well,' says Tania, 'if there's travellers, I'll not say "no" to a gift. Bring gifts! A dance, perhaps.'

'I'll take a golden helm,' says Egon, 'to protect my brain.'

'I'd take a fleece,' says Marcel, 'but I've an allergy. How's about a skin? A flayed one, no longer occupied, like our neighbours down the South used to clothe the priests. I see myself, descending from above, quite hieratic, with a prophecy – "Outface nature: drop! You won't be like that smithered egg, you'll drift."'

'Some prophecy!' says Tania. 'The guys in the plane...'

'Where should I go?' I ask.

'You idiot!' says Egon. 'That's the point of travelling, that no one knows where you're going.'

'Nor where you have been,' Marcel says.

*

'I shan't talk to anyone, if I go,' I say. 'They're all ahead of us, in modern things. Peasants, monks and fishermen. All the stuff we've mulled over – food, the sun, gender, all that – they're living through, or they have passed. The rest is their jobs and cash. I'm not interested in all that. I'll be a tourist, just like Clara, silent.'

'There's landscapes,' says Tania.

'No,' Egon says, 'there's not been those for at least a hundred years. There's fields, maybe, and planes – though not the sort that fly.'

'Well, what's for him?' asks Marcel. 'He's silent, doesn't see and doesn't talk. His inscape is the Empty Room. He's got no cash – it's not investment hopes that drive. No pills to sell, so humanity's not in view.'

They stare at me. I say, 'It's travel. What it's all about. Not war, not sex. I'll travel – maybe I'll look out for gifts, or maybe not.'

I wonder – maybe Hugo hopes the deal they made – the multicoloured friends, the bourgeoisie, the digging, and all that – will all come down. Then, his hopes, his reality will come. It's a vision. He won't see it, and he won't hear the cries, suffer the breaking up of everything. I say,

'If you voyage now, they tell you what to see, and what to feel, what everything is worth.'

They know all that.

Tania says, 'Of course, I can be anything. That's why my crap jobs don't bother me. That knowledge isn't satisfying, though. I want to go beyond the black square, beyond representation. Beyond the crap I'm in. It's not about voting for things. Nor people. It's seeing.'

'Yes,' Marcel laughs. 'Being caught in that, the black square – it's a devil.'

'The devil is, it needs a frame, to stop it from escaping,' Tania says.

'Travel is aleatory,' Egon says, 'or is meant to be. But now we know – chaos has its theory, to dream is not

escape, it's just a smaller room. Chance is the same –
everywhere in the universe, it's like the light, standard
speed, you can't avoid it.'

'Take some seeds. Small animals too, if your pockets
can...' Tania says. 'Repopulate.'

'Maybe I should take a person,' I say. 'It used to be
the deal, when people thought the wisdom of the rustic or
the seer was of some account. One to listen, one to write it
down. But now, you'll never meet the guys who matter.
I'd take you, Tania, but you're fey.'

'You're pretty fey yourself,' she says. 'What do you
expect from girls? Management skills? Besides, I
wouldn't share that plate of beans with you.'

'You're lucky if there's plates,' I say. 'And those
beans you plant yourself.'

We argue on, until she goes to whirl some more.

'I couldn't leave my room,' I say. Of course, I mean
'leave the bird'.

'I'd look in on it, just now and then,' Marcel says,
and laughs. 'I can't stand feeling I'm responsible.'

'We could be tragic heroes,' Egon says. 'They don't
feel responsible for anything. Their ingredients – foreign
wars, rivalry, envy – they're all around.'

'Let's keep away from civil war,' says Marcel. 'With
that, we might be on different sides.'

'You idiot,' says Egon lightly. 'If we're heroes in a
play, we already are on different sides, or else it's simply
dull.'

'Betrayal?' Tania asks, sweating, stopping the
movement, 'You don't mention that. Marcel's prepared
for it. He would neglect your bird.'

'My idea is this,' says Egon. 'Photos. They're a tiny
flash of time. Then they get fixed up, so's they're not

even what they were. They're tumbled into art, I guess, or out of anywhere they once belonged. Those shacks beside the track, long-legged birds with diamond trails as they take off, the warrior, his painted head... his Harvard t-shirt not in frame... You could do all that. Without the glass and machinery. Snap, snap! Future and past. You needn't take a bus – just snap in your head, you snap the picture. There it is! You're free not to move, to settle in the Empty Room, and, like the poet says, "drink down remembrance in long draughts". That way, you fight the war that Hugo fears, regrets it didn't happen. Photos in your brain: don't leave home. Wars that's really civil.'

'Yes,' I say, 'it's brilliant. It's like the cow, who's in the field or not, when I stop thinking of her. The problem is, no one can see what I have snapped, or even know if in my head I've touched it up, and prettified.'

'Oh well,' says Egon, quite offhand, 'you're hung up on what other guys may think. Ideas may nestle in your brain for years – and no one sees or hears them, then – out they come. Or not. We're made like that, you idiot: we live in there, above our neck. Memory, composition, all the shapes, the colours... stacked in there. They're only yours – but they're the same as everyone's. There's the advantage, and the limitation.'

'Oh,' says Tania, 'I like other people seeing what I do.'

'That isn't it at all,' says Egon angrily. 'That's you, and your desire. Not mine. The cataclysm that I'm waiting for – it doesn't yet exist – but it will come, you see the numbers run to meet each other, see them swirl like starlings in their flock...'

'I'm with Egon,' Marcel says. 'Even if in civil wars we'll be on different sides – though no one knows how many sides there are. It's like religion. If you don't see what is invisible, you are unworthy of respect. So let it be with mind photography. Let's have some samples,' and he turns to me. Maybe he covets my skin, cured like a suit of tan, bone buttons, ready off the peg to strut the town...

'With some practice, you could make a movie no one can see. And I can star in it,' Tania says.

'That's cheap, Tania,' I say. 'You've no spirit of the hypothetical.'

'Hugo's crowd,' says Marcel, 'always swims with the majority. Then, they're reviled for trying too hard.'

'You're an elitist,' Egon says. 'A democrat maybe, but with a taste for bossing other guys. Hugo may have got the message wrong. Perhaps he tired of being kicked for being right. You should live up to your role, the story that you're carrying.'

'Well,' says Marcel, waving fists, 'you're the reactionary. When it's all gone down, you'll build it up again, quite clean and pure. A Taj Mahal in honour of a whore.'

'Big prisons,' Egon says. 'All over this continent. Not gulags, perhaps.'

'That's where your militias will come from,' Marcel says, looking wise.

'No, no, you're all wrong,' Tania says. 'It's all prices and information. When the crop fails, the boss hands out the guns. Not here, though.'

She says to me, 'Take your photos now! The trouble with everything – is sequence. One thing after another. History. It honours resistance. Overcome it!' She dances off, shouting something.

The place is noisy, and they push us out, into the wet street.

'While you're gone, I could stay in your place,' says Marcel.

'Absolutely not,' I say. 'The last time, you pissed on my books.'

'They weren't on a shelf,' he says. 'They were all in a box. A little box. I'd drink taken.'

'And I hadn't left that time either,' I say.

'There was that book – *Life*. It pissed me off. The idea. A big fat text,' he says.

It's raining hard. 'The photo,' Tania says. Beneath the wool, you can see every crease of her body.

'A light, in the sky,' I say, looking up, grimacing. 'A star is born. Or dead. So very small, and yet they say – "Oh, the distance. Oh, the power. The kilometres across, thousands, millions – the gas, the dust. Those figures – you can't get them bigger, or you'd not believe in them."'

I add, 'Tania will stay in my place. If I'm not leaving.'

There's a good feeling between us all, although – it's true – a civil war, and we'd be on different sides, not even considering how we view our destinies.

'Another photo,' Tania says. 'Quick.'

'My friends,' I say. 'A group of tough guys, laughing, smoking. there's a dog, one ear dangling down. I think they're building railroads, running an ostrich farm. Maybe those are ammunition boxes.'

'Smoking, drinking, a dog – that sets them outside the culture where I'd thought you were,' says Egon. 'And in back – those boxes Marcel shouldn't piss in.' He laughs.

'Come on!' says Marcel. 'Maybe those guys are in a cartel. Or vigilantes.'

I think we know the details haven't come out well. Maybe there's a black flag, not the flag of Azawad, somewhere on the wall behind, the calligraphy so intricate, so beautiful. They're all friends to each other, in the photo, though they don't rate friendship very high.

'It's Africa, South Africa,' says Marcel. 'They are prospectors.'

'I don't see it,' Egon says. 'Forget the dog, the cigarillos. North Yemen, perhaps. Those high houses, the structure picked out in white, like skeletons. A marvel.'

'Power to the people,' Tania shouts. 'We could all have joined in then. We were much too young, of course. We were unborn. I told you, it's exactly that: too soon, or else too late, always before or after.'

'Tania,' says Egon. 'You know, Marcel uses you.'

'Of course,' she says, 'I like it. It doesn't mean I'm weak.'

'I can't have relationships,' I say, 'but I like seeing people play their parts.'

'People!' says Egon. 'Watching them – that isn't tolerant or understanding. People are water going over falls.'

'My suit,' laughs Tania. 'It's shrunk. I couldn't get it off, even if I wanted.'

'I could dry you off, Tania,' I say.

'Your place?' she asks. 'It's a dump. It smells.'

'I know,' I say. 'It's temporary. I'm on indefinite leave.'

'You're fired!' says Marcel. 'Well done indeed!'

Marcel can pull important strings. Egon – his office makes forecasts, angles on the future, just like Tania. People are impressed, then they forget.

Tania? Friend of the powerful. Probably a tease. A confidante. She listens, doesn't join. Doesn't join the other women either – that's quite suspect, I suppose.

'I have no religion,' I say. 'I have no animals, no state, no country. I have no hostage, no arms, no drugs. I have no pleasant place awaiting, no family, no comrades. I'm clean.'

'Yes,' says Tania. 'That's the way. Not taking anything from anyone. Not even food stamps.'

'Come on, man,' says Marcel. 'Everyone has lots of everything. Now, or later.'

'Going outside,' says Egon. 'Outside the history of the place you're in, is squalid. It starts macho, and ends begging.'

'I'm not reactionary,' I say. 'I'm better on my own, without explaining.'

'Everyone says that nowadays,' Marcel says. 'It's dull, like favourite foods.'

It stops raining, so we can go into the pub again.

'We must decide how you get to Azawad, and be sure you're on the right side,' says Egon.

The whole idea gets heavier.

'Those photos,' Marcel says. 'They're what you want to do.'

'You know what they say,' I say. '"They become what you don't want to do. Photography kills more surely than bullets", and "Every time I snap you, I lose you a little." A little bit flakes off. That's what they say, and it works, however committed you might be. To a cause. Either as photographer or model. In the photo those two are one, a bit dead.'

'Kills is rather strong,' says Tania, easing off her suit and drinking schnapps.

'No, I follow that,' says Egon. 'Something kills, and it may as well be photography. It's an accessible record, after all.'

'I'll ease off the photos, then,' I say. 'They're scattershot, unless you're certain of your cause.'

'Waiting for the crash – it means we're not embattled people,' Tania says. 'We're waiting. It's quite a cop-out. Maybe not a crash – instead, there might be – a rift, a shock, a quake.'

'Tania, one day you'll find yourself alone against the French army,' Marcel says. 'Their *képis* wave unsteady in the midday shimmer, like doves pecking at corn that's soaked in booze. Me, I'm at their head, like Custer. Except – I'm not going to his end.'

'Marcel gets dropped in awkward zones,' says Egon, 'and sets some guy up to be hacked down.'

'Tania's not a confidant,' Marcel says. 'She's an informant. Individual spies – they're rare and cute these days. Spying's mostly done by big machines. She isn't innocent. She coaxes, and out drop secrets, wrapped in cloth of gold. Their price is good.'

'Oh come now,' Tania says. 'I'm an innocent, perhaps the only one. Everywhere's a state of siege, so you're afraid. Don't betray, don't compromise, just toe the line – if your enemies don't get you, for sure, it'll be your friends.'

The barman says we're shouting. Maybe he knows where Clara went.

'Marcel!' shouts Tania. 'You kill people! For the fucking government! I thought you were just a diplomat!'

Marcel waves her away. Egon says to me, kindly, 'We all know each other's trades. It's not as if we were somewhere extreme, like in Jenin, that's really under siege. We must accept each other, and discount the rest. Tania too.'

'Is that what you think, Egon?' I ask. I don't care what he thinks. He doesn't reply, but gestures to me that the barman's beckoning. Something about Clara. 'If they fall asleep,' the barman says, 'they don't get let back in another time.'

*

Later, we're in my room, Tania and I.

'Surely, Tania, you knew Marcel's diplomacy gets him dropped in interesting places?' I ask. 'Places where they are about to fight? Where we used to visit.'

I put on a disc: the girl on it shouts, 'I wanna be the girl you die for.' I could love her, easily.

Tania says, 'The course I did – scaling walls, diving through fire. Walking up hills at night. It doesn't seem useful now.'

'Everyone starts courses,' I say. 'I'm too wise to get caught in that.'

Tania knows all our secrets. Egon makes his forecasts – dire, until they tell him to go easy. Then, it really is getting dire.

'Who can you trust?' Tania asks. 'Well, Clara. I love her. Hugo. So what? Him and his bird.'

'Clara's like us. She tramps the world, and troubles follow,' I say. 'She gets plague in the womb.'

'That's gross,' says Tania, laughing. 'She's a good sport.' It isn't so.

'You're quite pure, Tania,' I say. 'You sell information, but don't betray. It's just profit and loss.'

'It's honesty,' she says. 'I don't invest in futures. Let the eggs fall. Clara travels, so they think you want to stay because you like some place. Then they deport you, quick.'

'That's where Clara went?' I ask. 'Somewhere else? Jail?'

She doesn't react. 'This space thing,' she says, turning off the disc and looking briefly at it. 'Conquest and escape – and building cabins in the skies where guys don't need to change their underwear. You know – I'm glad the only thing that people see in me's the colour of my hair. It lets everybody spare the words.' She picks up a pencil and pokes the bird. 'He has the right idea,' she says.

The bird's not happy with her, right idea or not.

'Those photos, yes,' I say. 'Marcel and Egon – they both want to trade in gold. And those prospectors – that's what led Custer on, and did for him.'

'Oh,' she says, 'there's no glister in a Custer,' and we laugh.

'If you need a job,' she says, 'Marcel or Egon – they could get you one.'

'They don't much want to. Nor do I,' I say. 'With Marcel, you give a sample of your blood. A double. Egon – gives you a pencil to draw curves,' and I take the pencil away from Tania. We stand, wondering about sex. She takes my hand and puts it over her heart.

'You see,' she says, 'this will mean the death of me. Now, it's silent. But soon, one day...'

'I'd no idea,' I say. 'You seem quite indestructible.'

'Egon says, to push on, ever faster. Compete. Last battles may be victories. In the end, you go too fast – but when? It's like my heart,' she says. 'Maybe today. Tomorrow, maybe. Forget the probabilities, drive on.'

I say, 'Marcel wants to try me out. He says that I'm his Tonto. We'll drop in somewhere, try to make some friends.'

'One day, I'm sure, you'll say which side you're on. And what you do,' she says.

'Maybe today,' I say, 'I'll tell. Tomorrow, maybe.'

'Everybody here, who's not into money, is about to rule the world. That's the big business now,' says Tania. 'Me – I might have a kid. I can't wait to have her read to me. The sea over there, us in a garden of aloes, she'll be reading Malcolm Lowry, and the sun will burn up everything we don't want to see.'

'It's a bold choice,' I say.

'Well, lots of women do it,' she says. 'Not everyone has kids already grown and literate.'

'No, the book,' I say. 'The book you have her read. The text, whatever you may call it.'

'It's right that everyone should know, every life ends in a death, and in a kind of burial,' she says. 'Every mother should pass that on. Forget the stuff about purple Bols for breakfast, and meeting dukes or having cash, or fathers in a trailer park.'

'Even so,' I say. 'It's not an easy future you've laid out.'

With a gesture, she crumples up her leggy daughter and the book. 'My work has people in it now,' she says. 'Millions. One more – she wouldn't register.'

'Gaming?' I ask. 'Those war games?'

'Oh, it's geopolitics. We do the battles. Make the little soldiers from some edible stuff. When it's over, into the pot, we make a stew,' she says.

'Like those old guys, play with Trojans, Confederates, all that?'

'Oh, much more serious,' she says. 'We slog it through. All the future. Fight it with figures. And figurines. Of course, we put on weight – samozas for aeroplanes, flamethrowers spurting tabasco – it's a feast. Why stint ourselves?'

'You could do Armageddon,' I say. 'A lay version, naturally.'

'Oh yes!' says Tania. 'That we do! Battalions of chives, and officers – the fat and greasy ones – *porcini*: then there's staff – the *cèpes*. And simple ones, the privates – *chiodini*.'

'And you set them up, figure them out, with your brainy friends?' I ask.

'Not exactly: I come in at the end,' she says.

'You cook them? Dead, survivors, the whole mess?' I ask.

'Oh, I'm not the cook,' she says. 'I do the other necessary things.'

'That's how you know Egon, then,' I say. 'He does forecasting too.'

'Quite differently,' she says. 'Austere. He sends his people to the races – especially when there's ostriches. To teach humility.'

'Each in your own way,' I insist. 'Is bound in to the future. Marcel too – dropping in to make alliances.'

'You're not a pacifist,' she says. 'No one is now. That's how it goes. Trust me, my dear.'

Tania and Egon – both work for agencies making forecasts for the future. You find what it will be, then try to change it.

*

When I next see Egon, I ask about the ostriches, racing.
He's irritated. 'Who told you that?' he asks. 'Of course,
my guys go to the track. All kinds race there. Your chance
remains the same. Round they go, dogs, bikers, pacers,
like beetles round a stick. Even Daytona – my best friend
runs there. A Challenger. Ostriches – they are aggressive
birds. A toe can stab you to the heart. It's because they're
deep down lizards. Animals deceive – I bet yours sings
like Valkyries when you aren't at home. But racing –
that's not forecasting. It's just fun, and fixing. The
future's all arithmetic – your health, how long and how
you'll live. How you'll die, what you'll have read. Your
social class. It's numbers, nothing personal.'

'The future seems banal,' I say. 'I guess you needn't
make it really happen, and have a plan for after. It's just a
guess.'

'Oh no,' says Egon, even angrier. 'What would be
the point, analysis without a plan? Of course they do what
we foretell. Why wouldn't they? Why wouldn't we?
Besides, the stuff that Tania does. Cuisine! They're
predators, those guys, hunt with their mouths, eating the
rarest things.

'They gorge, and then disgorge. They're foxes.
They're not hungry, but they go on slaughtering – sip and
suck. They don't understand, that what they think is rare
is merely repetition. Gold sought so greedily – it's the
same stuff, anywhere. In the end, their grub is all the
same. Those guys consume the earth, and say it's delicacy
that drives. It's death wish, scraping wombs, eating the
larvae...'

Egon talks on. He's right, I don't dissent. His empty
room grows darker with the dusk, the wires trail out the
sockets, birthing cords. He talks of thoroughbreds and
soufflés, fuel injection and purées. 'Your food will come
from rocks,' he says. 'We'll pound it out, like oil. You're
right. It's oil, everything, it's ancient leaves composted
down with shit from dinosaurs, you dine on cannibal mice
who've passed through pythons' bowels...'

'Those battles Tania's crowd enact?' I ask.

'We do that too,' he says. 'The tons of ravaged flesh
– surely there's some better end than burial?'

'I see it's all connected,' I say. 'Numbers, the facts,
the knowability. Yes, it makes a connection. But does it
make a sense, a whole? An allegory, possibly, each part in
turn allegorising some other part?'

'Well,' says Egon, eager, latching on. 'An argument I
had with Hugo, about – "the death of beauty". Hah! We
grasp that. But it's meaningless. We grasp, we grasp,
tendrils, daffodils... Full of meaning even when quite
meaningless.'

'Yes,' I say, unable to follow. 'You're on to
something there.'

'Take Marcel, now,' Egon says. 'We think of
dropping him, it's like a bomb – that's quite the American
way. Except – he's not a bomb. He's just a smarmy guy,
wanting to make a friend, economise. That too's the
American way, quite improvised and unpredictable –
except that things you improvise – mostly they fall apart.'

'You've turned off our path,' I say. 'You're into
something else.'

'No,' he says. 'It's contradiction, knowability. The
knowing of what's there, and what is not. Take Clara,
now: an explorer. Finding things, that is her goal. She

disappears. She seeks – but now it's she who's lost. The onward thrust – turns to despair. What she seeks – suspended, invisible, not seen. And she – maybe she's not anywhere at all. Like Armageddon.'

'In a lay sense, of course,' I say.

'What she seeks,' says Egon, slowly, 'is in the future. By definition. Her future. What Hugo seeks... is nowhere.'

'You're playing, Egon,' I say. It's dark here: 'We can go to the Empty Room. Tric-trac. Dice. I'll beat you.'

'Maybe you will,' he says.

*

'You guys keep coming back,' says the barman in the Empty Room. 'You must think we sell a potion...'

'Of course we do,' says Egon. 'A *Zaubertrank*. We'd not come back unless we thought we'd be transformed.'

He talks to the barman, about Daytona, his girlfriend, boyfriend, who races, who's an ace.

'No Tania?' the barman asks.

'She's cooking, I expect,' I say. The two laugh. 'She cooks for everyone,' says Egon. It seems that she's a boss. She's hidden that – deceit, or modesty... Spinning her tale.

'No one's here,' I say, thinking of Clara who's thinking of Hugo.

'You should have more interests,' Egon tells me: 'Psychology. Like Shakespeare was always laying out – alternatives, the puff and the deflate, the boast with bitterness.'

'Oh, I guess I'll try to pull it all together,' I say. 'You guys all laying down the future. If you weren't all doing it, you and everyone, it'd be worth considering. I don't know where to start.'

They make to turn away. I say, 'My take on time is not like yours. You see time and the future as the same; time trickles on, and that's the future taking shape, you're in it, then it's gone. I see it rather as a question: "How should I prepare for it, the future?" Which implies: it may not come. And how might I prepare for that.'

It doesn't stick with them.

The barman seems quite sober.

'The problem is,' says Egon, leaning close, his hair inlays shining, the breath dark. 'My forecasts, if they're right – I still shan't be here to see them, garner up the praise.'

'I see that,' I say. 'The temptation is to get them wrong, and screw the gullible.'

'It's true the good guys always win, however long it takes,' says Egon. 'Mostly, though, mine's the frustration, knowing the unknowable.'

Daytona's in his eyes – not the race: the afterwards.

'It's like Marcel,' says Egon. 'He complains the guys he talks over to his side – aren't really friends. But then – what if they are?'

The cases don't appear symmetrical, but Shakespeare surely could have lined them up.

'Well,' I say, 'I come from terrible scenes. That's my excuse for lounging here.'

'That's true,' he says. 'That's worst of all. Being shut up, not even one of them, your fellow cons. Those tents, the sacks of kibbles you're supposed to eat... Take a drink after – you explode! And tortured too, no doubt. And you, quite extraneous – I'm sure you told them that.'

'I told them everything I knew. That brings humility – so little that you know; and even that is not enough, it's not a drop,' I say.

'Well, maybe they weren't that interested anyway,' says Egon, drinking more to show his affect, his worldliness as well.

The barman says, 'I asked this banker guy if he'd been to jail. I needed money, and they have a store, they give it to you. You need a relationship...'

'Bankers don't think of prison, I'm quite sure,' says Egon.

'Oh yes they do,' the barman says. 'All the time, they think of it. The males – with them, it's jokes and kisses, but you do them wrong, they send some guys. They're really violent, in the street they're animals. The females do the paper stuff...'

'And did you get the cash?' asks Egon, not much interested.

'Maybe it's true,' the barman says, pulling Egon towards him, bending him over the bar, yanking at him to disengage the feet curled under the metal rail. 'You get your funding from the track? And never leak the info to us, who serve here, and obey?'

'Of course,' says Egon, freeing himself. 'It's done so everywhere. My guys – they used to jockey, drive the motors. Now they're at the track, making our fortunes.'

*

Here's Tania. She seems angry, and she says to Egon, 'You rat on me, my dear – I'll burn your soul, so's when you get to hell, there's nothing left to pinch and torch.' She shouts some more.

'Tania,' Egon says, 'I didn't know you were religious. Too much faith is always perilous. Agnosticism – that's the flatline, suits us best.'

Tania turns on me. 'Your trauma, that we don't know what it was – a crash, a revolution, some virus? – should be cured by now. Into the spin again! Work, plan and plot!'

'You've all come a long way while I was outside,' I say. 'Before, it was peering at the future, now – you're quite familiar with what's to come, parading up and down.'

'You know what comes next,' she says. 'It's not "the striking of the hour that spells revenge" – all the moralistic stuff. Changing it, what's to come, is more demanding than the understanding. Hugo could have told you that.'

'It all goes on around him, unchanged, Tania, as he spirals out,' I say.

'Fuddyduddyfoo,' she says, sticking out her scarlet tongue at me. 'You're deaf, just like your bird. You should try this for him –' and she flutter-tongues, 'thrrrrrrrrr!'. 'You should hear the new sounds – first electric, now generated in the space between your ears,' and she laughs, drinks my drink, turns back to argue with Egon.

'It's not what we want that happens,' she says, 'It's not will, not existentialism, not ants lobotomised, running in their free paths. It's not Nietzsche, not knowledge in the dusk.'

She's vehement, has made this speech before. They both ignore me. Egon says, 'What happens may depend on Marcel, the deals he cuts. That leaves us out. Besides – we all live hugger-mugger now. The poor have their poor socialism, the rich gold-plate themselves. We must be free from happenstance... and yet, the spindly carts still trundle down those hills set in their clay...'

'No,' shouts Tania. 'They try to trundle up the hills. That's why there's smash.'

They circle round. Egon says, 'The unpredicted destroys the future.'

Tanya says, 'You must make it yours. None. The. Less.' She turns to the room, proud, a better queen than those there's ever been.

The barman points at me: 'This guy,' he says, 'Listening in. Maybe he needs a beating.'

'I'm not sure,' says Egon, looking moderate.

'I don't want a beating,' I say. 'I come from equivalents. Kiss or tell.'

'And he's a coward, too,' says the barman. 'Likely he controls some resource, badly.'

Tania's laughing,

'No, I just don't want a beating,' I say. Maybe that makes me a coward.

'Tania,' says Egon, ignoring me. 'You're not a corporation. So you won't rule the world.'

'I'm not a continent either,' says Tania, showing teeth, 'but I'm desirable. Greatly so, Egon, and you're not.'

'Come on!' says Egon to the barman, 'I'll wrassle you for the bar.' They strain, hands clasped. 'OK,' pants Egon, 'I'll yield.' The barman laughs, and Egon wins, slamming the guy's relaxing paw down hard.

'I'll get the deeds,' the barman says, emptying the till, pushing the takings in his shoe and limping out. He waves to me, as he goes out. 'This guy here, the coward, he can run the place now I'm expelled.'

'It's not my thing at all,' I say. Nothing's resolved. We help ourselves to drinks.

'Corporations are just bad gods,' says Tania. 'They kill you from inattention.'

'That's an easy take,' says Egon. 'It's like – "you can survive anywhere if you've something to eat and they aren't after you".'

'That seems right to me,' I say, but they don't hear. 'You two have trouble listening,' I say.

'We have to deal with big tough guys,' says Tania. 'Bosses, ministers, generals and such.'

'I thought it was arithmetic,' I say. 'Your jobs.' I didn't ever think it was.

'Well,' Egon says, 'maybe we just like the theatrical stuff. It's not about to disappear.'

'I'm traumatised,' I say. 'That's why I don't speak loud.'

'Tell us,' Tania says, 'but none of your soup, your minestrone spiel, your great system, made of erotic pasta shells. I hated *Star Wars*.'

'Last summer,' I say, 'I went to see the desert flower. When it rains – there's jewels, pink, blue and red, scattered all over, and there's trees like rhubarb, sages beneath their massive leaves, each with a story that will stick to you, each stickier than the last.'

'Were there others with you?' asks the barman, who's returned, forgetful of the past half hour.

'Experts in sand – guys who sought it out for glass, for fritware, just bottled and for sale. Yes, there was a woman too – remember, I'd gone to get away from Tania – our story had a writer's block...'

'It's news to me,' says Tania, pushing me away. 'No woman I. Never a button I undid before this gentleman.'

I go on, 'It was a kind of taxi we were in. You know, the desert isn't flat like you would think, it's lumpy, and it didn't rain. One stretch is like another, and we stuck. We'd vodka, but no water – who'd put water in the drink? And it was hot and thirsty weather. We sat there for some days.

'Then, some guys on camels came, and there was this grand hotel. They said, "We'll put you up for free, but you must be true seekers after desert flowers, and desperate as well."

'"We are, we are," we cried, our tongues as thick as parrots'. "If we could have flown....we'd not be importuning you, our hope lies not in states, nor laws, but in the sky, the rain... we'd fly..."

'"Here, no one flies," they said, "The sky has one unique sign – it is the sun. No bird can flap across it. In that sign, maybe you'll conquer – or if not, you'll burn and desiccate... But here's your rooms."

'It was indeed a grand hotel. Upstairs, they housed old Bolsheviks – I saw Bukharin, hanging out his sign – 'Do not disturb' – and there they were, Sverdlov, Frunze, Ter-Petrossian, some playing bridge, some diving in the pool. The guy who's on reception said, "There is a chapel of a kind, 'reflections on the Stalin era', if you want a moment on your own..." And so there was, not much frequented, we found out. And other wings, all full of rooms, and guys you thought had disappeared. "And up the road," the guys, receptionists, they told us, "there's another hotel, grander, for the Right. They have the lovelier women too, but that's the way it goes," and so it was, though there's no sign of road. And in the other wings, there's guys like us, who've come to see the desert flower, and have their trucks break down – brainy boys and gals, phenomenologists were there, philosophers of every stripe, and liberals and bankers too, each keeping to their circle, but the vodka came in jerrycans, the pools were laced with it, the food was like they had before the '14 war – you heard the geese, the boars, the ostriches, all tethered in the yard outback, quite proud and waiting to be slaughtered for our suppertime, and making little happy sounds...'

'Some of those guys sound like they should have been in the other hostelry,' Egon says.

'That's what we said,' I say, 'but they said it was overflow. Commercial deals.'

'And then you got the bill?' the barman asks.

'Out further back, there was a sea of grain,' I say, 'although it never rained, it ripened there. It seemed quite alien, but there we were, all day and night, a-toiling in it, bringing in the sheaves, as you might say. My comfort was the woman from our minibus. She stroked your head, the waves of corn went flat, and like a grassland, guys were playing *chalumeaux*, and you could smell the snow up high somewhere... The toil, that was to pay our keep – it seemed quite just and equitable. Then we were kidnapped...'

'There was no point in that,' says Tania. 'If you couldn't pay the bill, there was no cash around.'

'That's what we said,' I say. 'The possibility was, to sell us into slavery. We tried it for a time, the digging and the sweeping floors, and building monuments, and railroads too, until we heard some guys decided they would start another empire – then, there it was, the French army all around again, and those old Bolsheviks in the upper floors, they fought them off, long muskets, flags, and manifestoes too...'

'And you joined in?' asks Tania. 'So you really were a Tuareg,' and she looks admiringly.

'Well, obviously, the outcome was unclear. We didn't see the future, so we don't know if it works. But evidently – we escaped. At least I did. My love I left behind; and all the precious things, the manuscripts, agenda – I couldn't carry them, or even make a list...' I say.

The memory is heavy. I shall never have that same experience again...

'Did you see Marcel?' asks Egon.

'For sure, he was in a wireless truck,' I say, 'though they use computers now, to tell you who to shoot.'

'And Clara?' he insists.

'Clara's on humanity's side,' I say. 'She'd be pitching tents somewhere, digging latrines...'

'I must find your tour operator,' Tania says. 'They seem adventurous. It's all plausible, except for the affair I didn't have with you. Your woman, the nameless one... did she disappear?'

'Her religion didn't let her get involved with me. It's all quite recently been systemised, encoded, and enforced,' I say.

The barman says, 'That story is as tall as those rhubarb trees you didn't see, my friend.'

'It wasn't rhubarb,' I say, resigned to be disbelieved, 'Just to give an idea you untravelling guys would understand.'

They're silent.

I say, 'That's why I'm still tensed up. But, since I know the scene, they'll call on me to mediate – I know the complicated web there is out there, how it's sorted out... I'll be a plenipotentate.'

'You think too much about Hugo,' Tania says.

Then Marcel comes in again. 'I can't say where I've been,' he says, unasked. 'Arid resorts, important scientific work, a friendly power... I can't say more than that.'

'We'll drink to absent friends,' says Egon, and, abundantly, we do.

*

I have a vision of my bird, lying on his grit, and on his side, quite relaxed, one eye open and one shut. 'What should I do?' I summon Hugo up. 'You idiot,' he says, 'Get another bird, make sure it's not a female, and enjoy the music.' The vision disappears. For sure, the bird is fine.

'You're almost cool,' Tania says to me. 'All that culture, a hundred years of history, it all slides down around you, and there's famous heroes, dead as bricks, that's shooting round you – and all you bother with – is your stupid fucking bird.'

'Oh no,' I say, 'I do reflect on things. If it's the future that you're interested in – why don't you change how you behave yourselves right now? Oughtn't it follow, that what's going to happen – maybe you can't change it when it does, but you can make it happen differently by being different right now?'

'That's pretty adolescent,' Egon says. 'If we behave different now, who'd know what its effect was?'

'He makes the point,' the barman says. 'Better than I've heard it put this week.'

'It was all quiet,' I say. 'Still, and cold, waiting for the rain. It was like Hölderlin, those sheep bells – no sheep, but there was tolling, carillons, or metals clashing, with no measuring of time. You understood what it might take to fill a space, immense, and live in it, quite passive, not suffering. Better than to move, to walk, to clamber up the glass and fall back down.'

'Those grand hotels,' Marcel says, 'they'll find some rich guys, fill the emptiness.'

Daytona ends – five days nonstop. 'I've won,' shouts Egon, 'though, alas, I must celebrate here with you.'

'Your pilot,' Tania says, 'she should bring our gifts.'

'I could buy this bar,' says Egon, 'though I guess I'd have to put in seats, scrub the graffiti.'

'Hold it!' shouts the barman. 'There's still an ordinance in force, "If you're not with us, you are with the terrorists." Remember? That holds for time as well. I'm in the present: you guys – you're in the future. Then, we may be poor and hungry – that terrorises, don't you see? You guys – you're responsible. The cops are on the watch, I've put them on alert.'

'We have our own cop: Marcel,' says Tania, improvising a dance. 'As for me, I can tell you who'll win wars.'

The barman makes the sign that gets you rid of witches.

'Winning's like Daytona,' I say. 'It doesn't bring the gold. Though maybe there's skin suits for Marcel here.'

'If you're afraid of what you're going to see,' the barman says, 'other guys will get afraid. Like me. Maybe you should pack it in. Watch the lady dance right here.'

'The forest's full of wounded animals,' Marcel says. 'Who's going to bandage them? The stamping and the bellowing! For sure, not all of them survive. Me – I want that tan suit, some guy's sloughed-off face, and stick it on my own. That way – I'll frighten, or I'll pass for someone else.'

'Marcel,' says Tania, 'you're no use at all. You've lost your fear – now you've got too bold.'

'Oh,' Marcel says, 'I'm on a mountain ridge, high above your smoke, your smell, the things your eyes can see. I see you people emptying out. Banal exchanges. Or – false beliefs. Sometimes you're victim of both those, sometimes of one or other. If I fall, down from my ridge, on one side, there's blue demons, on the other – your empty shells. See...' and he struts along the bar. 'I mustn't fall...' and he walks on, nothing sustains him, he's a metre and a half above the floor.

Gently, he descends, assumes some gravity, glances at us all, challenges to conquer fear and do like him.

'I hide my body in the dance,' says Tania, responding to some question that's not asked. We feel we're empty people, filled with false beliefs.

'You're lucky you're not young,' says Marcel, 'and don't need invent a world quite new, where you lay out your flesh to have your comrades eat and spit it out.'

'That'd be new stuff to fear,' says Egon, turning delicately away.

'No, no,' says Marcel, 'you conquer it before you have it. Fear'd be just another thing to be despised. That's maybe the best. To you intimidated guys, though, it's a suicide.'

Tania's dance comes to a pause.

'Of course!' says Tania, 'I'd forgotten. In the future, there'll be new people, absolutely new – first, the young ones grown, then others, with no beginning and no end that we can see. I'd thought,' and she says to me, 'we'd put you in one of our scenarios. The future! – but you'd maybe seem like that space cat. Dead in the past, dying in the present, dead in many places, and circling here.

Maybe, going on in history, always dying, always dead. I'd not inflict that on you just to show our cleverness, our prevision.'

'The young guys now – they don't talk and act like you, like us,' Marcel says. 'They have their planet. There, you've no time. There's pictures, and being in the show. Being cut, bleeding, and disappearing. *Pierrot le fou*. And that's the brave ones. They've already fought, Tania: you can't put them in your wars.'

'Clara's son,' says Tania, 'was filmed, raping or being raped, or both. He did it all himself, a star in his own snuff movie, a suicide without a cause.'

'Oh no,' says Marcel. 'He lives! Just click on to him!'

'Perhaps it's not the depths,' I say, 'it's just the deepest he imagined. It's not like a real death. Only a tiny cinema.'

'You guys,' the barman breaks in, 'you flap around. You go from corpse to corpse, and squabble with each other. How can you sketch out the future, if you don't know how things work? Analysis! That's what you guys don't have.'

'What's yours, my friend?' asks Marcel. 'Those words aren't new to you, I'm sure.'

We laugh. The barman says, 'You promise terrible things – ends of this world and of that, and just the opposite: ships that run on sailor's breath, houses inflatable, all that... It's all annihilation! Who are you, where are we? You promise us disaster, or a wonderland. There's your power, but where's your title? We, the deserving poor...where are we, while you make your hypotheses? We've disappeared, we're glittering ghosts, we change our shapes and colours, live in no place, a shower of space dirt, always flowing – now flood, now fire, now boneyard, *place d'armes*, or hall of mirrors... The struggle – nought availeth!' He stares at us, helplessly. 'It's chaos without the liberty it brings,' he says. 'To keep upright and vertical, we have to bury our old selves... we're ever reborn, intimidated, impotent.'

He gifts himself a shot.

'You're as ambiguous as anyone,' says Egon. 'Shapeshifting. Enjoy it. You needn't bury yourself, just cast off your old threadbare skin, feel fresh and clean in your new suit.'

'Exactly,' Marcel says. 'Put yourself in the other guy's skin. It's the first step to seeing and doing something new.'

'Whatever's new,' the barman says, 'it isn't made by us.'

'Us?' Tania says quite angry. 'This is "us", right here before you. Empty glasses. Waiting for the refill. Ours, the foretelling, and the making it come true!'

We're all quite drunk. I think of Clara. I avoid thinking of her son – I'm not a moralist.

Marcel's whispering to Egon, 'That barman is a pain. I hate these pseudos, think they're sceptics, but really, they're ignorant. Lazy too.'

'And drunk,' adds Egon, and it's true.

'You can't get rid of him, the pain, in here,' says Tania. 'Park him through that door, where it says Blanks, where Clara's son departed from...'

'Marcel,' says Egon, 'I disapprove your methods – but approve the consequences. Go to!'

'It doesn't need be me,' says Marcel. 'That takes the step. The guy undermines our commitment, is all. He doesn't know a thing.'

'He said he'd been to the cops. These guys always look for contacts, get themselves known. He could be Chechen, who knows,' says Egon. 'They all have blue eyes.'

'He's poisoned all of us,' laughs Tania. 'Him and his mates all over town. This booze!'

'Everyone has a sad history,' Marcel says. 'When we come near the end, everybody drags their sack of bones.'

'Come on, guys,' I say. 'Absent friends! There's Clara, and there's Hugo. This guy's not a part of them. None of your business.'

'Don't romanticise the barman,' Tania says. 'Be just. He's not living on a buck a day. We're not the stereotypes – it's him.'

'Don't send him through the Blanks,' I say. 'You're not like that, Tania. He's done nothing. Don't joke about.'

'Yes,' she says, 'the Blanks. That would be anomalous. But – he's done nothing. Nothing much. Not yet. But I don't see you knowing what I can do. You're not that interested, in that kind of thing. Knowing people, their psychology. Or stopping people doing what they do.'

'It's not about me,' I say. 'If you go after him, who'll pour our drinks?' I try to raise a smile on all of them.

'If it comes to that,' says Egon, 'I can do that, easy, pouring.'

'Tania, there's a nastiness around...' I say.

'Yes,' she says, 'Egon's nasty, I'm nasty. The barman too. You're not so sweet yourself. When we're all dead, others will come, being even nastier.'

'I need a slash,' I say, to the world in general. I don't go near the 'Blanks', its karma stinks. I'm quite drunk, sober enough to know I'm drunk. The windows in the

Room don't open. I find a tube, let into the wall. I guess what goes in must come out somewhere.

'That's gross,' says Tania. 'It jollies you up, you needed it.'

'Where's Marcel?' I ask. 'And Egon? and the guy?'

'Marcel and Egon, don't you know how keen they are on one another? On themselves?' she asks.

'They just went off?' I ask.

'Now, hold on this,' she says. What can it be? A target pistol, a hash pipe? No, it's not a party, we're alone. It's some kind of fancy key, some pompoms on the end. She pushes me towards the door beside the Blanks. It says 'Fulles'.

Fools, *filles*, fowls? We are inside. She doesn't take her clothes off, but it's clear – the deal is cut, and then it's done. 'There,' she says. 'Done, and done well, quite well. And no stain left, on past or future,' and she laughs.

Egon and Marcel are back. 'Where's the guy, the barman?' Tania asks.

'Oh,' says Marcel, 'he had to go home, I guess. He left the key.' So he did, it's like the one with pompoms on.

'Tania,' I say, 'I didn't say I loved you.'

'Oh,' she says. 'Any time will do.'

'Hugo is right,' I say. 'You should do now what has to be done. You'd be a fool to trust people who come after you. Generations you've never seen, never instructed.'

'Are you sure you're not a patsy?' Tania asks. 'Even saying that?'

'I don't care what you think, Tania,' I say. 'I'll do it, what must be done, right now – not fool about with projections and extrapolating, like you do. Your procrastination.'

'My driver – she'll maybe do the barman's job,' says Egon. 'It's attested – she'll not win next time. It's in the forecast – she'll not race again. They let her keep the helmet – that's my gift, my golden helm, as I foresaw...'

'Shall we see her shining out in you?' Tania asks. She surely can't be jealous? And she's not curious.

'I'm the colour of Roquefort,' Egon says. 'Lia's a brown shade, that soaks up oil and dust. She comes from Guadeloupe. Or Guatemala – I always forget. Lots of murders there. She doesn't feel a thing.'

It's unlikely Lia wants to stand behind the bar for ever, watching us get drunk.

Here she is.

'It's not just drink, Lia, with us,' I say. 'Tania and Egon – they're important guys. And I – there was a shoot-out, but I'll start off again soon. You should come over by me – I live alone, with a bird. In a cage.' Lia laughs.

'Is that your line?' she asks. 'Your psychology sticks out. So, you're quite prominent!'

'It interests me,' I say, 'where you're from. The social question. The violence all around.'

'Oh yes?' she says. 'Do you really care about those working classes, the peasants and the rest?'

'First you know,' I say, 'then you act. Or you don't, and feel bad. Even worse than if you do.'

'I prefer driving fast,' she says, 'faster than the rest, so you don't have to look at them. Coming last too – that's not so bad. It's a comment, after all.'

I think of Hugo, and the book he used to press on us. 'The development of capitalism in Russia.'

A classic. The ground on which to act, first or last. I say,

'Did you really win Daytona? If you had, you'd not come here...'

'The key is, to find the level of importance you want to function at, and then stay there,' she says.

'Rich guys worry about what they're breathing in,' I say. 'Their air. The noise, the insects for the birds to eat. But it's the structure that matters, whether it creaks. Has it reached its end?'

Lia looks at me, dead eye. 'The air I breathe is rich and nourishing,' she says. 'It's from refined dino shit.'

'Come on, Lia,' Tania interrupts, 'you didn't drive – you laid the bets for Egon, then collected.'

'Any idiot can drive,' says Lia. 'It's only fear that holds you back from coming first.'

'It's rather trivial, don't you think?' says Tania. 'But I guess it keeps you in high heels.'

'Talking of guessing,' Lia says, 'you guys were pushed to do your homework, passed your exams, gave right answers – then, there was nothing. Nothing left you wanted. So, you futurologists, you spend your life just doing schoolwork. Reports, sentences. Work. "How awful life will be" – unless we do our homework. That's your future, not mine...' and she talks on. Tania pretends to move away and talk to Egon.

'Fuck it,' says Marcel. 'How'll we drink with that Lia, clacking like a fighting-stick?'

'Egon and Tania, they're the kind that plan the future, then they get loaded on to trucks and dropped off in the estuary from the helicopters,' Lia says. 'Nothing. Nothing is left. Only their absences require that it's other people praise them, weep for them.'

'They're not political,' I say.

'It's not what they say they are, it's what the others think,' says Lia.

'It's only ritual, what they do,' I say, going part the way with her. 'They're oracles, stoned maybe, but other guys must bleed out in the sand.'

'You hang around them,' Lia says.

'The future here's the only thing that moves,' I say. 'The present's just a waltz of molecules.'

'I've got some bumblebees your bird might like,' says Lia, moving Tania further out the way and pouring me a Manhattan.

'I never suspected he might have a dietary hangup,' I say. I turn to Tania. 'How'd they deal with the barman?'

'Oh, Marcel would've taken him up, shown him how to parachute. The next time, they'd have given him a 'chute,' Tania says.

I say, 'It's in terrible taste, what those two did.'

'Oh well,' she says. 'You need to learn – complicity's the rule of life. Besides, you'll never tell – those seconds of freefall – the most important, the most orgiastic of your life! The secret revealed, the whole earth coming up to you, to embrace, to be one with you. You hit – you've had the experience, but no memory of it, ever. It doesn't hurt, it's the beautiful conclusion, better than you could imagine. Isn't that perfection? The supreme experience, epiphany, revelation – and no recollection, ever. Isn't that what we are after? Everything comes true at once, finally. The end.'

'Those Manhattans will help,' says Lia. 'If that's what you want. But Tania's right: complicity. With yourself, with everyone else. Lets you lose yourself, sink into the big unknowns, sip at ecstasy. That's the supreme feeling, the universal human good. Takes the edge off, lets you chum up with the gods, worship your teen idol, back the least awful, start over, say "better next time", "I've learned the lesson." What could we do without it?'

Lia and Tania hug. They're friends, you see it at once, even for those who don't believe in friendship.

'You guys are high on the Tuaregs, I gather,' Lia says, polishing glasses, dropping some: 'They're pretty bright. When you race over their bit of sand, they charge you some dinars. And don't give me Timbuktu and old books – they're illiterate.'

'Oh, we're keen on all that,' says Marcel. 'We'll do the expedition. It's all set up. This time it'll come out right.'

'Watch Lia!' Egon says. 'I love her, and we'd take her with us. But – she's like those ladies on the rocks, making eyes at Ulysses. Human form – but without a human substance.'

'That's rather good,' I say. 'Anyway, you must expect, enchantment has a price. Me – I'm a sucker for sirens.'

The bird is interested in the bumblebees. He doesn't eat them – each is half his size.

Next day, Lia wears a long buff coat – a brewer's apron, tan, colour of her skin. It covers her, she's quite invisible. 'A present for Marcel,' she says. '"Remember the old barman?" he asks, and of course I don't. That way, I'm covered up, the service is discreet... He says we should rent an Everglade, load us in, go to the Tuaregs, see what they do, which side we're on. Are we the new ones – or is it them, a new empire, nomad soldiers, a persuasive creed?'

'Really,' I say. 'I should go down further South. Unfinished business. We visited all the other places, when Hugo was younger, of course. He'd been banned.'

Maybe she's being mischievous, and mishears. 'A band?' she asks. I say,

'Yes, over the world, singing "Our many-yeared life, like flowers, like dust and shadows, ending..." Made the groupies cry.'

'There's this smell of future all around you lot,' says Lia. 'Why the Tuaregs?'

'Oh, I guess – a huge marginal land, where many other territories join,' I say. 'A people marginal, at the limits of everything – everything that's old and new, and profitable. The French, the Chinese, the rest... And everything that's stirred up, running to and from the North and South, trying to settle everywhere.'

'Everywhere not settled,' Lia says. 'And everyone who's sick and desperate and longs for causes, new life, old life... I love that.'

'Americans there, of course,' I say, 'they have it deep inside – discovering more Americas. Dealing with the Indians, painting churches white, taking slaves and freeing them, and trains at three o'clock with corpses on the seats.'

'A little future there,' Lia says. 'A study for you all, the experts. The infertile, emptying and filling up with desperate people.'

'Yes,' I say, 'though I'm more interested in the South. But – we were all Tuaregs once. Nomads. Look what's happened to them now. Our core, our heart – it's been smoked out. We started so. Is that the end for us, where they are now?'

'There's not a bit of you that's original, or genuine,' says Lia. 'An end marks a beginning.'

'It's not that easy, Lia,' I say. 'You're bringing in quite other stuff.'

'It's that easy, with you guys,' she says, and laughs.

'My room is full of bumblebees,' I say.

'You're not supposed to have the window down, not when you race. I did, and they came in. They've got quite rare. Take care of them.'

'They can't get in the cage. The bird – he watches them,' I say.

'They're like in that movie, where the helicopters are coming up the river,' she says.

'We shan't see landscapes, that's what Tania says... I guess we seem quite colourless to you, Lia. We're scholars,' I say, unconvinced: 'Even so...'

'Tania should leave her hair alone,' says Lia. 'That way she'd seem less short. She's right – I haven't seen a landscape, not for days. Now, we'll need to pack the Everglade. Guns, documents – and drugs. That's what you need to travel round and trade.'

'I guess they'll want to put the Tuaregs in camps. They're not called camps. That way, they provide for them, until the cash runs out – then they don't know what to do,' I say.

'That spookie type, Marcel,' says Lia. 'He'll get us there, and think of guns.'

*

'We're always returning, always at least thinking of it,' I say. 'Painting our pictures, colouring our faces. Down

South, you know, they've got capitalism. Like Russia, long ago. And now.'

Later, Tania enters, kisses me. I see she has some lipstick on a tooth, the colour of her tongue. She asks, 'And what will you do, Lia, apart from drive us?' Lia struts up and down in her tan apron. 'I'm famous, Tania. And I entertain. And now I make you feel so ill with drink – you have to come back in and do it all again. And you, Tania, what do you see, peering into what's to come?'

'Well, Lia,' Tania says, quite warmly. 'I tell them who to put in jail, how long for,' and she looks sharply at Lia and me. 'Who to go to war with, and if we'll win. It's no mystery, what I do. Egon tries to prove us wrong, and Marcel's there to see it all comes true.'

There's nothing Lia can say to this.

'You know all about Hugo too,' I say.

'Oh yes, we know about Hugo. He was rather sweet,' says Tania laughing. 'Doing impossible things in the past, then hoping they'd have turned out right. And you! Harmless, funny even.'

'So,' Lia says, pretending to wrinkle her brow as her brains discharge. 'You do a history of the future, all quite fixed.'

'No, Lia,' Tania says, sternly. 'Not *of* the future, *in* the future. Not all the detail's solid.'

'Well, Tania, spill it!' Lia says, juggling a shot glass. 'So's we can learn our parts and act it out.'

'Lia!' Tania laughs, 'that stuff, the information files, costs cash. A huge amount. And if I told you everything to come – see, it wouldn't be the future, it'd be now. The present. That's the catch.'

That's the secret, then. And – it shows Tania and Lia, with their to and fro, after all are friends.

'Still playing boys and girls, then, Tania?' Lia asks. 'And happy families?' They kiss, and Lia says, 'You've lipstick on a tooth, my dear. You look like you've eaten someone.'

Women have always interested me, much more than men, though I've no wish to switch, not permanently... I think of Clara – she'd a son, up to a point. It's dangerous, to have a family. You reproduce – and you are vulnerable. But if there isn't one – it's much the same. You can bear arms, children... everything, it makes you vulnerable.

*

Marcel shows us his new find: it's a fat dense discus shape, mauve – Brazilian agate, set with emeralds and topazes. 'What is that gruesome thing?' asks Tania.

'It's worth a lot,' says Marcel. 'And it's unique. It's false – the base is plastic, only the jewels are real. I bought it off a guy... And, you know, we're not keen on the Tuaregs. The Kurds though – more people quite invisible – we love them. They're sat on oil... This here,' he waves his object, 'is the colours of their flag.'

'Oh no it's not,' says Lia. 'I've raced through them. Nor is it Azawad. It's somewhere else, somewhere new. Mauve, brown and green. Nice. Nasty, rather.'

'OK,' says Tania. 'It'll be some new place. A country Marcel's invented, to be recognised, or cast aside. Maybe that's where your bird comes from,' she says to me. 'It's like a *coq de roche*. I never heard one sing. Maybe if he had a woman...'

'I told you, you're hooked on families, Tania,' Lia says.

'He's so small,' I say. 'I'd need to find a mate so tiny... and even then, there's no guarantee he'd sing.'

'You only want a singing bird so's you can be like Hugo,' Marcel says. 'Let it be quiet, if that's its thing.'

'It may be here illegally,' says Tania. 'Stolen, kidnapped from somewhere.'

'A *coq de roche* is larger, and it's orange too,' says Marcel wisely. 'But – it's time I told you, I've a problem with our trip.'

'You are our rock, Marcel,' says Lia, laughing. 'Our cock of all the rocks. What have you done, Marcel?'

'I stole,' he says, quite pleased and quite ashamed. 'They fire you if they catch you. I'd need to be consultant then. They have you kill some guys, and pay quite well. But... it takes a time to organise.'

'That seems quite picayune,' says Egon, who's been slumbering. 'Everybody loots. It's what you do, in foreign parts.'

'I took it off a desk,' says Marcel. 'Right here. And so, that doesn't count. No Everglade, poor Lia. We'll go separate.'

'That's not the deal at all,' says Lia, furious. 'My destiny is not to live behind this bar!'

'That was clumsiness, Marcel,' says Tania. 'Not at all like you.'

'It's danger, makes me do it,' says Marcel. 'Then, when caught – to justify, spinning it out, denial first, then face it down, and in the end, repent, enjoy the punishment, and rise again...'

I say, fingering the emblem, 'Aesthetically, Marcel, you've discovered the abyss.'

'There is another side,' he says. 'The guys who had the thing, the flag design – they maybe thought, aha! let's start another country in the sand, and make this its device.'

So, we'll leave, in some way. With an experiment, a country, in view...

My room, empty. The bird, wondering what's to come. Nothing. I can't take him. Even if he sings, it won't reveal... anything. He's stuck in my little room. It's anonymous and dull. Waiting for what's to come, a ribbon of time, a spool as tall as me. As tall as him – a couple of centimetres, in his case. Down South, in Africa, you went to jail for life, what could you do to leave? – sing, open the cage?

'We might engineer a country, yes,' says Tania. 'No little homebaked cells like yours,' she tells me. 'Everything a proper system, and everything custom-shaped, that works the best. Find the right people to put in. Or, if you're humanist, build it round the people, make them fit.'

'Hush, Tania,' Egon says. 'You're making like a stereotype. Compromise, respect. Not Hugo.'

'It's all speculation,' Lia says, unappeased. 'You might get a cook book out of it, Tania.'

'What else can we do?' Tania asks. 'You must have a plan. Even for taking a drink.' And to show it's not just rhetoric, she drinks.

'I can't disagree,' I begin. 'Something is better than nothing, philosophically speaking... Better prison for life than crack forever, on the street...'

'Don't talk like that,' says Tania. 'We want the best, not saving people.'

Later, I say to Lia, 'The only thing I'll leave here, in my room's the bird. What will become of it?'

I've some idea, of course...

'Here's what you do,' she says. 'You buy a quintal of those seeds, and leave them on the floor. It's paradise.'

'They'll sprout. There'll be a sea of green, and not a breeze to make the colours turn,' I say. 'Besides, I think he's maybe eating insects now.'

'Easy!' she says. 'The roof leaks, so there's grain. And Indian hemp, although the price has dropped. He'll learn to harvest. And to sell. Insects – there's sure to be those roaches. He'll grow strong, to fight them.'

'Then there's those goddam bees,' I say.

'Easy too – you leave the window open,' Lia says.

'Aha!' I say. 'That brings us back full circle, back to innocence. The bird will see the window, and fly out. That's what we do, it's freedom. In his case – it's death.'

'Oh well,' she says, 'if you won't listen. And – you guys,' she shouts. 'Who'll pick up your tabs? You've all been running one since I got in this skin...' and she flaps her arms and hugs the apron.

'The desert – it's not the bird's habitat,' I say. She polishes her tumblers, eyeing them to be quite sure there's nothing in. My problem's swollen while I talked with her.

Tania had said, 'That thing, the creature, it will die, while you are dithering.'

I told her, 'The new country too – no one will settle there – it's too ungodly, and the bank that sponsors it will fleece whoever passes through,' and she said, 'It's not a camp. It won't exist. We're into future things. We'll just set up a metaphor, where no one dies, and no one lives, and no one picks up tabs for anyone.'

I tell Lia, 'Tania will pay for me, pick up my tab. She is my girl.'

'Oh really?' Lia says. 'And they never paid the guy before I got to put his apron on.'

'They hardly could,' I say. 'I must be off before poor Hugo dies...'

'Oh yes,' she says, 'before poor Clara too, gone mad with burning winds, still looking for her son.'

'Marcel tells us,' I say, ignoring the provocations, 'his wasn't just a theft, not "the thing in itself", he said, but "for itself". Beneath its weight, there lay a bunch of papers, setting out a kind of garden, palms and aloes, coloured birds and creeping things, no doubt. Rooms for people too – empty, of course.'

Tania, Egon, and Marcel – they come to say farewell.

Marcel says, 'Look! This mask, will keep the sandflies off.' He takes the barman's skin from Lia, covers his face.

He looks quite like the barman.

'They'll call for us,' I say to Lia, when we are alone.

'Don't bet on that,' she says.

'The Tuaregs won't wait for ever, Lia.'

'They've not gone there,' she says. 'Marcel and Egon – they are drying out. And sorting out their sex. They sought a dry place, for getting dry – desert sand, like in the movies. Not in Africa.'

I say, 'Poor Hugo. Not even he could draw them in.'

I'm not surprised. Their interest's in the future, they've machines to look ahead for them. Those guys in Africa – they'll have to fight it out without our help.

'Hugo?' asks Lia. 'Who wants to drive for days to see a dying commie? Just be reasonable!'

'At least you won Daytona?' I ask, expecting other spoofs.

'Of course,' she says. 'I got to keep the helmet. Egon wears it now.'

'They could have said,' I say. 'They could have taken us, to some resort... Then, there's this tab...'

'Marcel got fired,' she says. 'And in that disc he stole, there is another country still to come. You're landed with the tab, meanwhile...'

... and Lia closes up the bar.

Later, she says, 'You owe so much – it's better that you buy the lot.'

So, I become the owner of the Empty Room. Marcel wears the barman's skin.

*

'Clara passed through here,' says Lia. 'Always looking for what she's dropped.'

'Ah yes,' I say. 'That son.' Lia leans across the bar, whispers to me.

She asks, 'Why aren't you down in Africa? Tania and Egon – they're not in some resort. They receive instruction. So does Marcel. All in secret things.'

'I know about Marcel,' I say. 'He's easy. Mister Awful. But the other two?'

'They found an Imam,' Lia says. 'It helps them to prognosticate, they think.'

'It's not my thing at all,' I say.

'No one would believe it was,' says Lia. 'Is it conversion that they want, or knowledge about stuff?'

'I want something new,' I say. 'Not old failures.'

'There's new things all around,' says Lia. 'Everything, like the sea, forever renewed. Hugo – he's not something new – he's something quite impossible.'

'I'm driven on,' I say. 'Like you.'

'It isn't going fast,' she says. 'It's winning.'

'That's exactly it,' I say.

'Why don't you liven this place up? A bird in a cage, some marionettes?' she asks.

'I don't want to encourage them,' I say. 'The clients. A bunch of drunks, shouting and poking pencils in the bars... Besides, you don't like taking cash. Result – we're destitute.'

'I thought you wanted that,' Lia says. 'No cash.'

'I do,' I say. 'No cash, no credit. Purity. With tiny optics. Measured parsimony.'

Tania returns. She's quite serious. 'I would be a heretic, and dance,' she says. She doesn't dance.

'Heresy's a big thing,' Lia says.

'This "public and private space",' says Tania: 'All my space is private. And I want it all to be public.'

'That doesn't seem to be the most important thing,' I say. 'Tania, you're lost. You know there's something you should look for, but it's not a thing you want.'

Egon says, 'The quest, the certainty – do you want to find the truth? Or be a certain kind of guy? It all seems quite monstrous to me. Being instructed, informed – it's important for where we might go, and what lies in the future – but all absolutely beyond me, as a personal thing.'

'No booze for me,' says Tania. 'That's for sure.'

'When I lived with a guy once,' Lia says, 'I used to wish I'd written the book of Jeremiah. The princes hung up by one hand, and the animals all around, among us...'

'Writing's changed a lot since then, Lia,' Egon says, heavily, 'and who you were as well.'

'Don't worry, Egon,' Lia says. 'It was a mistake, as you can imagine.'

'You guys just hang around,' I say. 'Studying other guys' religion – and never do you go to Africa...'

'Maybe it's not our destination,' Tania says. She turns on me. 'And you – your piddling fetish bird....' She doesn't know how to go on.

'Marcel's had a terrible time,' says Egon. 'It seems he was down there, in Azawad, wearing his mask against the flies – remember how it looked like our old barman? It seems the guy had come from round about those parts. There was a lynching... They hung him up, it seems; hung by one hand...'

'I'm sure he'll come out of it quite well,' says Tania. 'Not all captivities are the same. Now, Lia. No more sleeping together, you and I...'

'So, it's back to niggling?' Lia says, affronted. 'Some genius must have spilt that in your ear!'

Who hears all this? Who celebrates poor Tania's body, Lia's too?

'I didn't realise,' Tania says. 'The road I've travelled was a stony one. Ahead – I see more stones.'

'No landscapes, Tania,' Lia says.

'It's true,' says Tania. 'They don't figure in my future. But – I foretell. And so, I know what I must do. I don't plan, not cities and not bowers, nor think to build.'

Austerity attracts, but leaves us all without a word.

A message comes, from Marcel. Without his mask; he's crouched down in a cave. He makes the revolutionary sign, and mouths. He must believe the mask covers him, makes him invisible – like Egon thinks his helmet makes him invulnerable. Once, it might be so. It isn't now.

'Cash?' asks Egon.

There's no one else in frame. 'Isn't that a French boot?' Lia asks. 'Just poked in. Those golden eyelets, the leather from black thoroughbreds?'

'Well,' says Tania, 'there's all sorts there – there's French and Chinese, Russians, Americans – then, there's those who used to be there... Marcel must have a side he thinks he's on.'

'If you guys settle up, pay those bar bills,' Lia says. 'We could send him a contribution.'

'Marcel owes too,' says Egon. 'Besides, the owner of the bar here – he's a friend,' and he hugs me close to him. 'He doesn't stickle for a coupla beers.'

'Clara's the only humanist I know,' I say. 'Maybe she'd intercede.'

'Maybe she'd think that Marcel was her son,' says Tania. 'She runs, but always drops the ball.'

We don't much care for Marcel anyway. I go back to my room; this talk of levying cash for him unsettles me. I see my bird is paler now. You'd say almost an orange tinge. It doesn't seem to bother him.

The Empty Room – I see it as a place, set in a place: another place, within another place.

*

I say to Tania, 'The Empty Room – it seems it belongs somewhere else, another context.'

'That's like saying you're not here,' she says. 'It's meaningless. For sure, you're not with Hugo. He might have sorted it all out, but it's too late. Nor are you with Marcel – you don't go down there to look for wisdom – it's survival. New countries? – ladders to climb out of your hole... He must have suffered for that theft. The disc, the new land – those jewels will certainly have gone, stolen or pawned. The disc – worthless, but he'll maybe bargain, with whoever holds him in the cave.'

'You're gullible,' says Lia. 'I bet the jewels were false, the mauve bit – real agate from Brazil. That holds the value...'

'Nonsense, Lia,' Egon says, 'nothing is of value there. Only when you ship it out it's worth a bit. Inside – it's just like Tania says – you fight for your survival. A stick, a book, a sheet of tin – anything to protect. So much for Hugo, so much for flags...'

'The future is a restaurant,' says Tania. 'If all fails. Our maquettes as I told you – they are edible. New food – that's what brings the money in, with pictures on the walls and whores upstairs. There's sure to be a place for you,' and she pinches Lia's arm.

*

'We can make it here for sure,' says Tania. 'Survive, as it all falls down. We've powerful friends, no assets. We are safe. If Egon buys us out, my agency – he'll make no cash, and then I'll take him over. It won't cost anything.'

'It doesn't work like that,' says Egon. 'Look, your powerful friends – they make you vulnerable. They fall on you – they crush you.'

'I'm the strongest,' Lia says. 'I come first, because I'm swift: and if they want to fix the race, they know I'll convincingly come last.'

'My dear,' says Tania, 'you forget. You don't race, you pour. You'll deal in dope, in horse and snow – and then the snow will melt away, the horse will turn to grass – and you'll be caught!'

'It's all hypothesis, of course,' says Egon. 'That's in the present – the future is a better bet.'

I say, 'We all have empty rooms, of course,' but they ignore me, and it's better so.

'You guys – in America you have to say you love George Washington,' says Lia, laughing. 'But I guess you've always had to!'

'Do we rescue Marcel, you guys?' I ask. 'Or do we join him? The new land – it's supposed to be Real Life... Adorno invented that, you know. Hugo knew everything, of course, and didn't rate Adorno much. Real Life you really live when no one's chasing you and you've got stuff to eat.'

'It's the "how", how you get it,' Lia says. 'Stuff to eat. I'd go with Marcel, better than being here with you...'

'Down there, that's just the point. They don't know "how",' says Tania.

'It's worth a try,' says Lia. 'Tania, you're in the business of knowing everything – but only everything tomorrow...'

'Hugo was a polymath,' I say. 'But those there are today – they make mistakes, besides, knowledge of everything, everyone has it at their fingertip...'

'Yes, yes,' says Tania, pushing on, 'go on, and speculate. Marcel's a prophet on a rusty rock – or else he's being executed. We've no idea. Now, hold on to this! There's someone trying to force me out, and spreading stories – that I'm out of cash, or that I drink, or that I don't: a convert...'

Egon looks smug, and says, 'You take instruction, Tania, and it's natural they think your future's different from ours.'

'It's not beliefs, Egon, it's the drills. Soon, we'll all be tired of it, I bet. And having answers ready,' Tania says. 'I should take Lia, go down there, and see if Marcel's needing help, or just recruits.'

'What am I, then, in your scheme?' asks Lia.

'You drive,' says Tania.

Lia's put out. 'That food you make,' she says to Tania. 'It's what the poorest people eat, and have to dress it up, so's you can't see what awful bits it is.'

*

They leave; and Egon says, 'Now! I've my future all set up, and hers as well!'

'What good does that do?' I ask. 'You've just got guys to pay.'

'No, no,' he says. 'I'm covered. They agree, or disagree, the future is uncertain, but ensured – you see, it cancels out.'

I have a picture, well inside, behind my eyes. Lia and Tania, arguing, arrive in Real Life State. The sign says, 'All deals done. Highest standards.'

There's the mauve flag, there the green stripe – an African pine, there the topaz... sand all round.

Tania and Lia, arguing still, outside the Beau Geste Motel. 'I hate the belle époque,' shouts Lia.

'That's your period!' Tania shouts back. 'Fast and horizontal – that's exactly you.'

There's a statue – someone, maybe Marcel – bearing the unknown barman in his arms. The place is too small for landscapes. Guys push at the fences, trying to get in, others heave the other side, and hope to leave.

'Yes, yes,' says Egon. 'Where's Marcel?'

'I've no idea. He's certainly alive or dead, or making up his mind which way...' I say.

This motel – neither real life, nor capitalism – I see people going in and out the rooms, I seem to recognise them all... It's quite a happy place, in transit everyone. The parking lot is full of motors with the trunks agape, guys selling booze from them, and stuff in gunny sacks, and sides of meat and lengths of things that could be carpets, could be frocks, full, empty; pick-up trucks with oily mounts for arms.

'Rooms' says the sign, it flickers 'No rooms' – but there's many, so many, rooms, despite the frantic movement, there are rooms for everyone. I recognise some saints and holy men, ducking in and out of each others' pad, some pelting with what looks like elephant dung, some embraced, their beards are intertwined, their twiggy fingers clacking in the air – such peaceful, tranquil air. Of course, there are no birds – except... not sun umbrellas, those, but creatures furled and vulture-like, blotched black and white, distempered worn-out rolled-up blinds, just hanging round and sharing in the fun.

'Forget the elephants!' shouts Egon. 'Are those vultures picking over Marcel?'

'It's like homecoming,' I say, 'or graduation day. Or end of school. It's all a celebration, coming to an end.'

'I don't care about them,' says Egon. 'It's Marcel. I'm sure he's on our side, though he does terrible things. And Tania, Lia too – I have loved them both, now one, and now the other, sometimes simultaneously. Where have they gone, where do you see them...?'

'That car,' I say. 'The springs have gone...ruined in those dunes! And Tania, I see her take Lia inside, one of those empty rooms – full as a hive with honey, until the dawn chases away the bulbuls, starts the two of them arguing again...'

'Oh no,' he says, 'of course, I feared this. Love... you spread it round, you cut it like a stone, you make it precious, and... it's borne away, it's set in some parure, some guy buys it for his guy... it is no longer yours, it's sparkling in the universal stream, it's cut, re-cut, table, trap or rose...'

'Oh come, Egon,' I say. 'They're tired. Maybe they'll sleep, anonymously. Check out tomorrow, like two travellers who separate and saddle up – it could be Marcel's on the desk...'

'Oh no,' says Egon, 'That's just prettied up. They have to stay together, see if real life's possible...'

Regret, jealousy, nostalgia – prospects of happy lands, once visited – Egon crumples down against the wall. I lumber down beside him. His sentiments, his presence – all repel me. I say, 'It is like that, Egon, we must get used to it. Hugo dies, and Clara disappears. Vendetta's after Marcel, there's torture and sneaky tricks. Lia doesn't race. You steal Tania's livelihood, my bird sings when I'm not there. What can we do about all that? Not change ourselves – it's quite irrelevant.'

'Forget about ourselves!' says Egon. He seems desperate. 'We must go, find Tania. Oh yes, and the Tuaregs. That was the original, the quest, I remember. You didn't spot any, in that Real Life triangle?'

'Tuaregs don't use motels,' I say.

Egon weeps a little: 'It's all over for us too,' he says. 'And Lia... that week at Daytona. A force, a goddess.'

'I'll go along with what you're feeling, Egon,' I say. 'But I don't feel I'm done just yet.'

I remember, Egon wasn't at Daytona. He was here.

'If we were expressionists,' Egon says, 'we'd rejoice we'd heard the hooves of those horsemen, the ones of the apocalypse. We'd think we were clever, making faces, colouring our masks with blood. Sharp angles, cries and discords. But now – I feel such sadness, there's such quiet. The few – they sing, they wave, they disappear, but up the road come millions, eager, famished. Looking like yourself. There's nothing you can do – you're born, you have to scream, to show you live and breathe.'

I nod. I don't agree with all of this.

He says, 'You know, motels. They're exactly what you'd invent that would be useful for the Tuaregs. Caravanserai. That's what they are – you see them filling up when it gets dark – Americans, you think. They cost too much, of course, for Tuaregs...'

It's true – the scenario, where everybody drifts away, there's quiet, tranquillity. Not peace – because around the bend, there's war. But overall, there's silence. Egon is wrong – those old guys had their warning, had their Caligari. They knew, and into the abyss they walked. We don't need another Doktor, no Mabuse, no Golem – we know all that. And silently, we walk...

'Hey!' shouts Egon. 'Wake up! We should go down there, and bring them back, Lia and Tania.'

'If they were there, they've left,' I say. 'Where do we start?'

'I'll give you this,' says Egon. 'The Real Life State is rather small. It's a place for overnights. My team, my experts – they can't say what future it may have.'

'If it was a republic for birds, a sanctuary?' I say.

'Would people come to watch vultures?' Egon asks. 'I doubt it. Or a parliament of fowls? Now, what's more appetising, is your red bird and his comrades, riding on elephants, chattering away, maybe imitating speech, darting in and out... Polishing tusks. Yes, that's the kind of colony that Hugo wanted – a touch of sarcasm, not that the birds could care... Showing how the animals can coexist. Your bird's too small to be hunted, I guess?'

'Well, not for food,' I say. 'Rather, trapped, sold into captivity. An enigma in a cage.'

'All these empty places, ephemeral settlements, these Azawads – history is filled with them,' says Egon. 'Not places in the mind, they're there, happy or sad. All with traffics, discourses, most with flags and documents, some guy on a throne...'

The idea attracts. 'And when they seep away, they're there and not there, like the empires and the faiths, no more, no less,' I say.

'I don't know about that,' says Egon. 'No more nor less than what? But I won't argue over it.'

'Everything is always present, Egon, and always fading fast,' I say. I don't know where this leads.

Egon says, 'Tania and Lia – you have a picture of them, but don't fool about. We're not into real and imaginary. Where are they? And Marcel? Down there, even where there's Hugo – anyone gets blown away by who knows who and who knows what – the most pretentious things the most unlikely, the campaigns unappetising... arms and sacrality, all confused... the happy land that's fertilised with cash...'

'Maybe they're holed up in your empty room, Egon,' I say, not believing it. 'Sorting each other out.'

'You know,' he says, 'don't exaggerate. I don't do complex stuff like Tania, though the effect is more appealing. I run bets. We take them on the future, and we make percentages. I can't lose, nor can the future – the principle's the same as Tania's, but it's more secure.'

This is no revelation, and it's easier than Hugo's scheme. 'I still don't like you, Egon,' I say.

'Oh, let's buddy up!' he says.

'Why's your room empty, Egon?' I ask.

'I could put in terminals – those sockets...' he says, 'but I don't even need a room. It's in my head. It's algorithms. That guy – al Khwarezmi, thought them up. That's his name in there. Choresmia, Khwarezm. Center of the world, that was, looking at stars – that's where the future lay, up there. But – they dropped the ball. I guess they shot at you?' he peers at me, to see if I'm still holed.

'Someone did,' I say, 'maybe they were French. All useless anyway. What'd you do with sand, except travel over it? Lots of places like that too – nothing much in them. Trees, parrots. And shooting.' He must have odds on everything, on me, on him.

'Did Lia win Daytona?' I ask him, as a buddy would.

'Of course she did,' he says. 'You could look it up.'

I could ask him – 'Are we immortal?', 'Did God lay down the rules?' – but he'd say, 'You could look it up.' It's not much use.

'In the old days,' Egon says, trying to hold me close to him, 'there were moral dilemmas, there was history – choices and catastrophes. Now, there's just distrust. Of everyone. Look at Tania! What she turned out to be. Marcel, staked out in the sun, manacled, decapitated, cut into strips by someone with the knack...' He looks sadly round. 'Then, there are syndicates, who try to break you, break the bank.'

'Do you distrust me too, Egon?' I ask.

'You most of all. You've survived. Or so you say. Maybe you didn't. Maybe you saw the worst, or else it passed you by. Maybe you're distrustful, just like me, of all enthusiasm, all passivity, the quick, the dead... the family, the couple, and the solitary, state or clan, the faith, the sickness...'

'You'll live for ever, Egon,' I tell him.

'No, no,' he says, 'you've deadly traffic in you.'

'Marcel did bad things,' I say.

'Oh, it was war,' says Egon. 'Besides, he stiffened up, skydiving, all that – and do you think bad things mean a person should expect, deserve a punishment? Worse things, done to them? Are we a moral tale, stumbling from badness that we do, to badness others do to us?'

'Yes,' I say, 'I dare say it's so.' I don't say, 'Egon, you were his accomplice' – it doesn't fit the argument he's laying out.

'I think this place should be a club,' I say, gesturing around the void. 'The bar – the barmen – they don't do so well.'

Egon persists, 'Marcel. A martyr. And he left a flag. Something to die for. For all those people, full of hate, mostly for others, but for their sad fate as well...'

'I'm not responsible for that,' I say. 'Go through the wrong door here, mistake the toilet, and you'll disappear. It's not my fault – the system got laid down long ago.'

'You need art in here,' says Egon. 'The question is – do you want to fill it up, or stress the empty?'

'There's your empty helm,' I say. 'And the flayed skin. They're empty, but you must look at them as if they're full.'

'People don't attack the strong places now,' says Egon. 'They let them fall down by themselves. It's the weak spots now – everyone piles in. That's what you should take from looking at my helmet – it's a protection that there's nothing to protect.'

'That's too arcane for me,' I say. 'The one thing we might do is – if Hugo's dead, someone should collect his bird... Maybe Tania's thought of that....'

'What crap!' says Egon, pushing me aside. 'This glass – it isn't full, it's empty, but it's still a glass. Take Clara's son – he killed himself, but he is still her son, and she's a mother too, for ever.'

'I know, Egon,' I say. 'That's casuistry.' I pour him a drink.

'A *Wunderkammer*,' Egon says. 'Accoutrements. Of warriors, putrefied and desiccated.'

'Did they finish their quest?' I ask. 'Did they rebel against their destiny, or smile as they trotted to the massacre?'

'That's beyond me,' Egon says. 'Now, who would join this club you're starting? Who'd want to join? Something like the Templars, maybe? Or a bobsled team?'

'Oh,' I say, 'someone who wants a structure.'

'No one wants a structure nowadays. Everyone wants out even while they make their fortune,' Egon says.

'You must have something, a wall to climb, a hoe to row,' I say. I don't much care. All the architecture hereabouts will be replaced, pulled down. Blown up, sometimes.'

'Clara's loose,' says Egon, gossiping. 'She's not a one for clubs.'

'I quite agree,' I say.

'Tania – she does things. Maybe she doesn't get them really done, but doing is significant. Even Lia – I guess although she drives, she's really driven. Other people hire her to do what she wants to do.'

'True. Like most people, I should think,' I say.

'So, where do I fit in?' he asks. 'Am I seeking? Am I a prisoner of some tale?'

'No, Egon,' I say. 'You're out of it. Your future's just a sum of probabilities. Odds and evens, all the same to you. You are an abacus. You click on wires.'

He's not dismayed. 'Well, that leaves us with Marcel,' he says. 'He's a warrior, he has a flag, he fights for this and that. Other guys – they go and look for him. There must be something there – he journeys on, places that's difficult. Maybe they'll strike oil. Maybe the blue guys'll all be put in reservations, if there's any of them left. But – he was there, on one side or another... Guys say they'll look for Hugo – they don't go. Marcel is different, he has company.'

'He gets his orders, then he runs,' I say. 'But – you may be right. It's not a farce, he's at the weak place where all gets resolved.'

When I last saw my room, the red bird was standing on the open cage. The door was open. I said to him, 'Well! And what if Hugo's bird should come and live with you?' He didn't flinch.

The door of the Empty Room – is opened by a blast. It's Clara – my, she's huge, a red sail, a pirate ship. 'I'm enormous, yes, I know!' she says. 'I'm pregnant with my son. It happens when you age, are discontented, surrounded by the dead.'

'Well, anyway, congratulations,' Egon says, trying to stand.

'You're both still drunkish, that I see,' says Clara. 'I guess that's why you live right here, clinging to the bar.'

'What news, Clara, from beyond the seas, beyond the bar?' asks Egon. 'Tania? – and is she dead, and did they bury her and mark the grave – a palm, its fingers upward pointing...?'

'Not her, not them,' says Clara: 'Marcel died. He has a second life. He lives. He's walking from his end, his sacrifice. He's in his second skin. He's walking out, the most unworthy, purified.'

'I'm surprised,' says Egon. 'In the ancient world, it was the women, nymphs and sirens, virgins, all that – who died at unjust hands, and then were born again, as if the sages couldn't waste a toothsome character.'

'Yes, yes,' says Clara, 'that is evident. But in this case, it's Marcel who's resurrected. Maybe they didn't know who was to blame for blowing him away – a kidnap ended bad, without the cash. Some friendly fire – who knows. All you need know, is he was killed, he walked away, and in some while he'll come in here... entire.'

'Not immortal, though, I hope?' I say. 'It happened once, but that's no guarantee...'

'I love it here,' says Clara. 'Or maybe I mean – I love you here. If only there were chairs.'

'I see guys leaning up against the bar,' I say. 'Not slumped. No need for furniture.'

After Egon – now Clara. I know – it's the emptiness attracts. I say, 'Clara! Remember *La Dolce Vita* – Marcello dumps his chick. He says to her, what she proposes, life together, is an "*abbrutimento*" – profound abasement. That's what I get from you. Away, away! Seek out your son, dead and happy now. The doors are there, both labelled – take your choice.'

Abasement. From Egon too, with all his bits of philosophy, misremembered all, quite unbearable.

She's overwhelmed: 'I didn't know you didn't care,' she says, aghast. 'Remember, though – we have a handle, a special hold, on Azawad. There, each has an insight, an experience...'

'The worse for us,' I say. 'For them. Hugo was right. Go to the end, the limit, the victory. The pips will squeak, repay your austerity with cruelty; they'll tear off your babbling head and toss it in the foaming sludge. They'll build casinos where you set your guillotines. So what. Do what you have to do.'

'Hugo – died like an emperor. An infusion. Bitter herbs, and bitter thoughts,' she says.

'His bird,' I say. 'I bet he left it. Squalid. Regrets for himself, a gesture solitary. Gestures – you should make lots of them. Die. Release your animals, have them run roaring through the town.'

'You petty bumptious petit-bourgeois,' Clara shouts. 'We had an understanding. You dump me – I'll thread teasels through your bones!'

'That's right, Clara,' Egon says. 'Make him suffer. He makes romantic deals with all the world – it's time the world fell on his head.'

Lia and Tania are back. They thrust into the bar, tumbling and laughing.

'And how was Azawad?' asks Egon. 'And Marcel?'

'Oh,' says Tania, offhand. 'We didn't get down there.'

'I had a vision, snapshot... there you both were, in Real Life Land,' I say.

'No,' says Lia. 'We were at the seaside. There were all kinds there. Arabs, Tuaregs, but no flags. At least – flags had a sexy name, they call them "bunting"!' and she and Tania laugh and hug.

'No Real Life, then?' I ask.

'Oh, lots of that,' says Tania. 'So much sex, we sickened of it, the sound, the smell. I couldn't face it, nevermore.'

'No, no,' laughs Lia. 'We plumbed each other out, consumed the mystery, flesh turned into flesh over and over, and then we were repelled by it, even the thought... I've taught Tania to navigate. That will be her task. You have a map, but often – I fall off the road, the craft goes in the ditch. That is our future now.'

It's Odysseus taking Circe on as crew. Are they sexed out, I wonder. Really? Their shoes are full of sand... 'The seaside's made of it,' says Lia. 'Now, don't have doubts that we are telling lies. That's where we went.'

'You should do some publicity,' Tania says to me. 'If Egon's taken on my job, I'll see to it for you. Not as a favour, of course.'

'Tania,' I say, 'everyone knows what bars are for. No publicity. No need for song. Maybe a dance...'

If, as I hope, the clientele is sparse and silent, it suits. Ending up – it needs thought, how to do it without sparkles or delinquencies. It leaves me to talk alone with God, and to decide which of us two will first fall silent.

'Yes, how is your bird, talking of silence....?' Lia starts – I say, 'That's below you, even, Lia, to mock the creature...' though I don't want to snub.

'The seaside's good for anyone,' says Egon. 'It's the sun's not good for you.'

'Son – I had a sun, too hot. Well,' Clara says, juggling her tragedies, 'explanations abound – my son was not an idiot. Was it the weather set him off? Or the artist's life, perhaps? I can't say I profited from his having been alive.'

'Of course not,' Tania says. 'Profit doesn't exist in many things. Take those Tuaregs – another country, or another people – quite in the wrong place. Geography drives you to be interesting, do what you do. And then the rest pile in: France, China, Saudi, everywhere. Friends of America. The trouble is – the rich guys love the bad guys, because the bad guys sell them stuff. The bad guys, though – they are real bad, incompetent as well. Then the rich guys back the rebels – but there's bad guys there as well. So, what to do? The lid is taken off, and underneath, there's good and bad. It leaves them speechless, those rich guys...'

We think of Marcel, balanced between the good, the bad – expect to see him walk in the door, maybe his hands tattooed 'good' and 'evil'.

'If Marcel was a hostage – what you do,' says Egon, 'is you must make contacts with all sides – that way the hostage has no human value, represents no qualities. The hostage is a chip – you play your cards, you win or lose.'

'Everybody always contacts everybody,' Lia says. 'That way you don't get hurt, and nothing's worth what you had hoped, and comes out warped. You – ' and she points at me, 'you are the only one who buttonholes creation. It doesn't answer back – but good for you! No deals, no compromise!'

'No, no,' I say. 'There's nothing there. There is no tongue, no word, no book, no song, and no lament. It's roots, worms, suchlike things, make an unseen territory. There's no intelligence, no brain, just stubborn tunnelling.'

'Hey!' says Tania. 'Hugo's coming – look, on my screen!'

There he is, waning and horizontal, on, it seems – a stretcher?

'My back,' he says, 'I reached up, to put his mealies in the cage – my back locked tight.'

A professional peers in on the scene, a nurse, perhaps, 'The back is seat of all emotions, speech as well,' she says. 'The patient cannot speak. He cannot love. However, friendship satisfies much more than love – you'll have his friendship, though in silence...'

Hugo talks on. 'I'll have these guys push me where you are. I'm sure you have an empty room. I'll stay, and give you my analysis. I think I've got it wrong, completely wrong, what happens here...' and on he talks. His face – peaky and pitted – man in the moon's. 'Yes,' he says, 'I see only the starry heavens from this bier.'

'Oh no,' I say, 'I can't have Hugo here. And Marcel's expected too – his long walk from the desert, what marvels, what disasters – no, I can't take both of them... Or either...'

'I think,' says Lia, 'we had the Tuaregs wrong, and all the complex issues that's involved. There's terrorists in everything, financial interests too. We'll get the deepest probe from Hugo, when he comes...'

'You idiots,' I shout. 'You were at the sea. What did you want – to help some guys? Grow up! – and Tania, you should have stayed prognosticating, eating your futures, maybe you would have been my girl...'

Hugo reappears on screen: 'If it wasn't for the money, those terrorists would just be bandits. With ideals, of course – bandits love their mothers.'

'There's so many poor folks to think about,' Lia says, 'I don't know how I'm going to have the time.'

'We're rallying,' says Tania: 'Over to Ulan Bator.
The future may lie somewhere on the way.'

Hugo is unstoppable: 'You know,' he addresses me,
'you ought to think of selling dope. I used to have
objections – but after all, you're already selling booze.
Dope goes down big, right here. The cheap stuff, and the
ritzy. Liberty – and pursuit of happiness. I'm stupid – I
don't see the connection. Liberty is liberty – that trumps
any pursuit. Not that you guys pursue just happiness.
Besides, it's the pursuit that keeps us lively, though you
can't call it happiness. The hunt, the race, pursuit – it
sounds consensual – but really – it's disorganised. It's
chaos. But after all, you can't all be the vanguard – logic
decides that for you – some guys will have to drop out,
some be last – so's to show the path is circular. I see you
as corrupter – that has its place, you need the talent...'

'You could repent,' Egon says to me. 'Join an order.
Take the vows. Hugo is right – we need to open up. Those
guys that lost an eye, or even legs – maybe they were
forerunners. I know, I know – not in good taste. But they
came back, seen and done all. Survived those wars, then
showed how sweet it was, to roam around, sniff the
forsythia, pluck the mallows...'

'Pursue the future, 'Lia says. 'It's always there
before you, and it must be happiness. And other things, I
guess. It seems the faster you pursue, the happier you can
get. But it's to do with being placed, up near the front, and
I'd not call it liberty. It's in the motor – that's what makes
the diff.'

'It's opportunism, all that Hugo said,' I say. 'What a
disappointment! At the end – it doesn't matter what he
says – but, he could make a stand. A little dignity.
Coherence.'

'I may have lost everything,' Tania says to me. 'But, suppose I love you?'

'That doesn't make you sound more appetising,' I say. 'But now – you navigate: you'll find the way for Lia.'

'Exactly,' Tania says. 'I'm in the car, but it's all for Lia. The right way. Her and the car.'

'That's how it works,' I say. 'That's the limit of a car, a journey.'

'You have property,' says Tania. 'The Empty Room. You bought it.'

'No,' I say. 'It cost a dollar. I just took on the debt.'

'It's the same,' she says, moving closer. 'It's yours.'

*

Marcel strides in.

'I did a deal,' he says, 'before bad things could happen. Then, when it was done, I had to walk, the longest distance.'

We stare at him. 'And did you see my son?' asks Clara.

'Oh yes,' he says. 'No doubt. Busloads passed. Hundreds, thousands of them, the people – all looking out the windows, not talking to whoever was beside them. Nations of them, every sex and colour, probably religions too. They didn't stop.'

'And – my son was one of those inside?' Clara insists.

'For sure,' says Marcel. 'Almost everyone there ever was. Passed by.'

'You were scared, I bet,' says Lia. 'Seeing those buses too, not stopping.' She hadn't see him falling from the skies, over and over, toughening his soul.

'You must show fear a bit,' he says. 'Or else they think you've got a plan. The thing is, not to challenge them, make your life worth more than your death, but in a way discrete...' and on he talks, as if he gets it from a manual.

'Which side were you on?' asks Egon.

'Well,' says Marcel, 'with my mauve paperweight, I had to found a state. A flag, a treasury. Those are the vital parts. That makes up Real Life.'

'The motel?' asks Tania. 'The trading in the parking lot? The people, moving through, and into rooms...'

'Yes,' Marcel says, 'that's it. That is a state. It was my guarantee – that I had some worth, was to be taken serious.'

'Tell us about the danger,' I urge him, though in my mind, I've seen the scene.

'You must imagine me – down South. The guys there are all good, whatever side they're on, but some are more good than the rest. Tourism's the thing, when the shooting stops, and the poverty has been contained,' Marcel says, as if he's reading from a prompt.

I see him, lots of guys sit round, they're sedentary, wearing spectacles.

'We talked a lot about the books, the scrolls – reading sweetens the soul, the breath. Reading is good, believing what you read is better still. It gives the word a value. Reading heresy, now, is quite a different thing...' Marcel has often told this tale before.

Behind him, there's a shelf of books: they're full of words, maybe The Word, and some are heresies of old, and some are stuff you read right now that once were heresy, and all are valuable, if you collect, or organise some tours...

'And stuff to pass the time, or give a sense there is design?' asks Lia.

'Look,' Marcel says, 'don't press me. I don't believe, and these guys didn't either, though we performed.... but reading is still valuable, and some books are worth more than the rest, and all have value, especially if you collect...'

I see where he's going. 'You mean, Marcel, you were a hostage of some librarians? Who decides the value of the stuff?'

'I call them archivists,' he says. 'To do the job, you needn't read, still less believe. But you can put a value on the stuff, see if some buyer pays your price.'

'And it works for people too?' asks Egon. 'This value thing?'

'Of course,' says Marcel. 'Hadn't you understood, every human being's valuable, and so they have a price.'

'So – you never saw the Tuaregs?' asks Tania, disappointed.

'They were always there, of course,' he says. 'In their little trucks, and some on bikes for motocross, and some on camels, I dare say. Good guys all, too – and some more good than others. But not in on the trade, the books, the tours.'

'Of course, there was anger, frustration,' Tania insists.

'I thought,' Marcel says. 'Of those lines – "one evening, the wine's soul sang in the bottles – Man, I thrust towards you, oh beloved and disinherited, from beneath my glass prison..."' Yes, man! I wanted a drink! A drink that wasn't tea. I thought of this, the Empty Room, myself propped up against the walls, with you, my faithless friends, listening to my tales. It made me strong. Frustrated too. And angry.'

'You see, Marcel,' says Tania. 'It's not too clear exactly what you did. We've an idea – about your theft, the barman, the founding of a state. Where are the gifts you'd bring us, if you kept us all in mind?'

'Oh well,' says Marcel, 'you know, there's always gifts. They follow on behind. And I remind you – how complex all that situation is – the bandits, the persecuted, the ordinary guys, the faiths, the resources – you'd for sure get bored were I to spend a day or so to sort it out for you – then, there's the landscape and the architecture. History as well.'

'Marcel – you're a resource all by yourself,' shouts Egon, embracing him, showing him off to us.

'Seriously, you guys,' Marcel says, 'don't think to go down there. There's agents of all kinds, and soldiers too, and guys who ask for cash – and nothing to be done by you, or anyone. Best not to think, and let the flag, my flag, float on...'

'While we are speaking of these serious things,' says Clara, 'what is the smell of urine here? The reek is not of death, not of my son – nor is it quite of life. It comes up through the heating ducts....' and on she talks.

'It's well known, Clara,' I say, 'if you drink enough, the sense of smell goes with the rest.'

Hugo sends more messages. 'There's only one of you who understands,' he says, 'one who took part in the past, and girds up for the future there – the guy who pours you drink, and owns the place and watches all and greets you when you might return, and hopes you'll leave and leave

him be. My associate, narrator, call him the knowall – to
him I bequeath powers of analysis, and fortitude, capacity
to resist the going wrong, the disappointment, and the
resignation. But – from him, you'll get no excuses, no
apologies – they're not worth the driest fig. His greatest
gift is, he knows the red bird sings, or may not sing. The
bird can: – maybe it won't. It's the last thing, it's what
you think of as the rest comes down... I'll leave a tape, to
show you how the singing sounds...'

The message comes and goes.

'It's storms that interfere,' says Egon, twining round
Marcel.

'It's empty promises again,' says Tania. 'It's true, my
enterprise of forecasting – it wasn't worth a lot, but kept
me well-employed and fed. Now, Egon's taken it –
financial raiding is the trick. You –' and she pokes me in
the chest, 'you'd better watch, Egon'll pay two dollars for
the bar and all your debts – and you'll end up as barman.
That's a risky job.'

'It won't be different from all the rest...' I say, but
Lia celebrates –

'Yes, Tania – you saved me from the barman's fate –
I brought the helm, and that empowered sly Egon here.
But now – I drive, you steer. The kingdoms of the
Amazons, along the roads where hoplites left their bones
– Asia and Africa. We'll rally on, my dearest Circe....'

Lia embraces Tania, primes her – it is time for
Tania's dance, for her farewell.

'Yes!' Tania says. 'I'll give you the dance of a
thousand dances. It holds the Odyssey, the Ramayana, the
Shahnameh, Amazon queens, the river Lethe... From the
first shufflings that we made to prompt the earth to send
up new year's shoots, then divas on the boards, wafting

like Diana's tree, bedded by princes – uncrowned princesses...'

And so it was. The dance went on for hours. The sufi interludes – they trumped the prejudices against dancing, and against women too – quite enchanting, quite ungendered. The dance before the hive was there: last dances of a species too, when the last one makes its count and knows 'I am alone, the last, it's ending, so much for the story of infinity and universe....' She imitates the lion, the elephant, the scarab and the scorpion... I walk around. I lock the Blanks, the Filles, put stoppers in the ducts and finish off the booze. It's over, the Empty Room is just an empty room, it has no future, absolutely.

I hear Egon say, 'Marcel, you can be the muscle, in the bets and in the forecasting. But I'm not sure – the bets, they come and go, like seasons. It's the future stuff, though: Tania's outfit – it bothers me. These catastrophes she invents, the wars that make things worse, when all the bosses said that soon we'd party... where do we fit in?'

'Well, Egon,' says Marcel, 'muscle is always needed, and that's me. You just keep on...The bets we'll take until the end. There's always guys with hopes and debts, and cash or credit for a stake. Have no trepidation, all will come out well, what you need to do is calculate the percentages you want...'

'You guys,' I say to Tania, Lia. 'I'd bum a ride with you. It's curiosity. I know you're bound for Ulan Bator – but you'll just drop me off – the countries over there are small. You hang a right to Africa, then I'll leave, after a bit, and head down south, and you go on. I might see Hugo, even bury him, maybe there's a testament... find mates for those two red birds, if that is what they want...'

'Look for my son as well,' says Clara, 'but don't send him back to me. Enough!'

Lia says, 'It's inconvenient. To make a detour, and to have a weight in back. That pert mute bird, taking in the view, and letting nothing out.'

I say, 'Tania was once my girl. She owes me something, that's for sure. A ride. And we'll soon, all of us, be absent friends.'

The Lotus

The lady with tickets for the football match wears diamond rings – some on the upper phalanges, when there's no room below. 'One for each confinement,' she says, 'though it was no compensation.'

'Which colour ticket?' she asks. There's purple and brown. 'It makes no difference.'

I choose brown, change my mind, 'Purple'. There's no difference. We're a few, standing round the pitch.

The visitors wear a silk kit, some have red hair. They're tall, they look Korean, or Kazakh, they arrange themselves in rows, like the mannikins on table soccer in a bar. They don't run, but kick out when the ball comes near. The other guys are short and sneaky. They have little boys, a lot, to plump out the team. They don't bother with a goalie.

'15–20,' says the lady at the end. 'Quite satisfactory.'

The tall guys drink the orange drink, and get back in the coach.

'Don't be afraid,' says the ticket lady. 'You've seen – everything has changed. Football. The rest, mostly.'

I say, 'I'm not afraid. I'm going to Africa. It's only Americans who worry me – the soft ones, the nice, the hard ones. The rest of everyone – no doubt they're the same, but I only fear the people I can see.'

The lady – Madame Feng – says, 'Your friends have driven off.'

She wears a brooch – it looks like ivory, and it says 'Liège'. 'Oh,' I say, 'they'll be back, they've got my bird.'

'Yes,' she says, 'it was looking out the rear. Its head and back – they made a question mark, and there was the black dot too – its eye – a little out of place.' She laughs. I ask, 'The tickets?'

'To see who was there, of course,' she says.

'It's not fear,' I say. 'It's the way they go on, blundering, trying to win. Not understanding.'

'Yes,' she says, 'they tried to fight a war. Terror! Anyone would be afraid, the black eagles up in flight. It was the prologue. They thought it was the play.'

'They fought a lot of wars,' I say. Of course those eagles fly, it's what birds do.

'Madame Feng, that's quite banal,' I say.

Poor Hugo, thought he had the future on his side.

I could stay here. Let the others take my bird. Give it water, and be done.

'It's shabby here,' says Madame Feng. 'France. But they're spent, those Americans. You could stay. Africa – they're still desirable, they've got something left.'

'Oh, I know all about the world,' I say. 'I don't take my worries seriously.'

'Those Beduin,' she says. 'It's a degraded life. Produces some results quite monstrous. It's not your world. You footballers! – you've earned enough to stay in my hotel, until your friends come back.'

'Difficult existences,' I say. 'They are a mystery. That's why they attract.'

'Not every mystery conceals a secret.' Madame Feng puts things into her plastic bag. The room she gives me has a wooden bed, a frame. She lays a mattress filled with grass upon it: 'There!' she says. 'There's the simplicity you've always craved.'

'You've got me wrong,' I say. 'It's true I kept a bar, quite minimalist. That's all exhausted now. I'm on the road. I want to see how old, stalled things might pick themselves up and run.'

'Ah yes,' says Madame Feng. 'You sporty guys! I've seen so many of you, legs identical, running like the beasts. I'm fortunate, you fit into my dementia, I don't need to discriminate between you. One does for all the rest.'

'While I wait,' I say. 'Maybe a picture? Over my bed?'

'My!' says Madame Feng, displeased. 'You are a precious! There was a picture, but of nowhere you'd recall. Invisible when you slept. Then I had it photographed, so's it would remind you of the picture. But what attracted me was not the desert with the tracks that disappeared. The subject that I loved – it was the writing up the side. That, you'd not understand.'

'That's mere whimsy,' I say. 'After all, the room is bare, and that reminds me of the bar, it has the desert and the tracks. That's also what I'm waiting for.'

'Yes,' she says, still offended. 'Be content with that. If they're coming back, your friends, they'll be here fast.'

She looks hard at me, my pallor, I suppose. 'You've the face of a *tomme*,' she says. 'One of those with a crust of black peppercorns, or currants. Black buboes. What's healthy in a cheese can be fatal – in you. I hope you don't mess my bed.'

I say, 'My work – mostly kept me from the sun.'

'Then, going to Africa's out of the question,' says Madame Feng, decided.

'Oh,' I say, 'I've seen all that. I know it'd be quite disappointing. It's the unexpected that attracts, the turn no one should take, that overturns the lot – the load, the destiny.'

'Yet still you long for the new,' says Madame Feng. 'And you're so vindictive! It doesn't help. You see, I'll tell you what three things can come about. Strategies, choices. First, there is nothing. You can't stop everything at 1922, with a new party secretary – waiting for transcendence. No, it's all to be forgotten, cancelled out. Nothing remains. "Nothing" goes on until even the memory, the hope, falls apart. It could end up positive or negative, war or stasis. You don't know, and so – "nothing". Then, second, there is surrealism. It's available to all. You have a tendency to that – I hear you in your bed...'

'It's the grass,' I say. 'The smell of the savannah, I hunt all night...'

'Then, there's the reign of the animals. Our survival resting on theirs,' she says.

'Well,' I say, 'these aren't exactly choices.'

'No, no,' she says, 'there's metamorphosis as well. Number three. Just toughing it all out. Waiting for what shape comes next. Like aging. A comic belly or a skullface.'

'You've a talent for analysis, Madame Feng,' I say. 'Where does that leave you?'

'There's the game and the hotel, the running and the lying down. That's what one mostly does,' she says.

There's noise outside; a black fog from a smoke-pot.

'Here's your friends back,' says Madame Feng.

Tania says, 'The roads were often blocked with stuff. And people too. Some cops, buying and selling guys.'

'Besides,' says Lia, 'we got banned, where the roads were clear. Because we made some smoke. Your bird – I fear it's black inside.'

'This here is Madame Feng,' I say. 'She was a high up, in the Chinese Party. Then she stole some cash, to buy this crap hotel...'

'This guy,' says Mrs Feng, 'tells lies. There was a shoot-out, that's for sure, he was involved – but not in Africa.'

'Well,' I say, 'I wouldn't go to Africa. How silly, out of place, I'd seem. First, I'd need to sort out the object and the subject: how they relate, how I'd take in the facts, and me.'

'Moreover,' Madame Feng declares, quite loud, 'I didn't steal, and if I did, I'd steal lots more than it'd take to run a scrubby bush hotel.'

'Don't worry, Madame Feng,' says Tania, 'we have a friend who stole. A flag – and made a country out of it.'

'I don't trust countries,' says Madame Feng, decidedly. 'I've never lived in China myself. I was in Harbin – as a tourist.'

'No problem, Mrs Feng,' says Tania. 'We're used to petty stuff, transgressions. Lia here, driving blind – there was a child, in the Banat. We didn't stop.'

'It was a chicken, Tania,' Lia says. 'And – I wouldn't care if it was you, Tania, who kept the whorehouse back in Harbin.'

'A friend stole my business,' Tania says. 'He made Lia here throw some races in the States. There, it's all over – and just think of the real casualties, everywhere. Those Americans, they have money to spread around, gifts of electronic hand grenades galore, all so's their own poor will have to work.'

'It's a mistake,' says Madame Feng, 'to have you guys taking trips to Africa. It's as you say, for you it's petty stuff, all cancelled out without a trace. But people down there have memories, you know. They'll remember you. You have a cloud that follows – all that fume...' and suddenly she's underneath the car, stopping up a hole in the muffler with a paste of fragrant herbs.

'Anyway,' Lia says to me, 'your crap bird sang.'

'Nonsense,' says Tania. 'It coughed.'

It lies down in its cage, showing its grey tongue.

'There's air up in my room,' I say. 'I'll give it what it needs.'

'Well,' says Lia, 'we wanted to learn about the world. Not just drive swift. We did. We learned – paranoid delusions and the madness of crowds – that sums it up.'

'That's just so trite,' says Tania. 'It's about unpopular guys doing everything to hang on and salt away some bucks.'

'Except for our tragedy,' Lia says, 'caused by old maps, and Tania listening to the wrong sort of music much too loud – *Le grand macabre*!... Not up to it, I fear,' and she pokes her tongue at Tania, a tongue grey as a parrot's, grey as my bird's. 'We had good times. The people were OK – it was the company that dragged...'

'Peace, Lia!' Tania says. 'No apologies and no excuse – just let us take responsibility – if either had some...' and they hug.

'Those guys,' says Madame Feng, easing out from underneath the car. 'Where you went, they have memories of a hundred years to turn to song and prayer. Just imagine – if you'd gone further on, gone South, and ever further East – there's thousands of them, the years, all bubbling still, with dynasties that left without a word inscribed, religions ingested and transmogrified... wars unjustified – no one survived... That would have slowed you down, you racing demons...' and she stands beside the two, a third grace, entwined.

'You guys,' says Madame Feng, assuming command, 'know lots of things. I see your talents – before you even boast of them. Your problem is – no place is good enough to hold you still. You seek an emptiness no urban scene can give, where you can roam like predators, and win your race – over and over, every day. Your future's very short – a stomachful away, no more. Here, you've a haven, here you can refuel. But all the rest – is motion. What you should be into – it isn't hunching over little screens and conning other guys, no, no...'

'Well, Madame Feng,' says Tania. 'What is our destiny?'

'Get into shipping, my dear friends,' she says. 'It's swift and clean. You drive the breadth of continents, delivering, collecting, sleeping at the wheel, following the ancient maps, at dawn you pray and check the tires, you fast, you pray again... outrun them all...'

'The work's all mine, I see,' says Lia, feigning umbrage – 'Driving.'

'That is what you most enjoy,' says Madame Feng. 'It's stopping that you hate, and do not need.'

My bird's recovering.

I say to Madame Feng, 'The idea was – to visit Hugo, his dream of happy lands, where, brothers and sisters all, we revel in our being species...'

'Stop!' says Madame Feng. 'You're maybe talking football. But – as for animals – you know, they often eat their young. And others' families...'

'Hugo saw conflict before the happy end,' I say.

'No, no,' says Madame Feng, 'I don't want that! No more in uniform. Those little blue caps, so unbecoming. It's each against all for sure, but not in lockstep... No! Survival. That will give us what happiness there can be. Doing what work there is, taking what shavings fall off the bench that we are set to work on... Remember the song – "He carries the child, the child who leads him, down the lonely road..."'

'That must be the child you killed, Lia,' says Tania.

'Did you give me guidance, a direction, Tania?' Lia asks.

'Now, now,' says Madame Feng, 'it's too late for all of that. Anyway, it's probably a metaphor. No quarrelling on minor things. The thing is: do my work. Deliver, get back safe, pay for the gas if someone watches, don't pay if there is no one there. It is of no account. Take your profit if you can, if not, it's probable they've robbed you.' She pushes on. 'Power? You guys – just look at you. You'll never have it – and besides, you must want something more, beyond it. Sex, cash? Forget Africa.. When it's rich, the rich will rule it – what do you expect? You guys – you're not into helping anyone. What do you want – to help the poor be poor? Get in your car – you can escape all that, the power, the poverty, the digging up the ground...'

'Madame Feng,' I interrupt. 'If you know all this, what are you doing here? With us?'

'I see things as they are, my dear,' she says.

'And what's the stuff we are to trek around on your account?' asks Tania. 'Not tiger parts, I hope?'

'You deliver, you don't pry,' says Madame Feng. 'And, by the way, don't tell your friends back in the

Empty Room: I've saved you from modernity. I give you meat. Your comrades way back there – they're hungry. Don't give them any scraps. You may not think it, but you three are all quite delicate. Well inserted too – no revolutionary stuff for you. Just keep your foot down, Lia, and you'll beat them all. Tania has seen the future – maybe you'll go faster than that too...'

I start to say, 'We want to play our part...' but Madame Feng is quickly in –

'You're too objective – change is all around, and none of it will benefit you guys. Think with your gut. Get in your motor, let the wheels do the analysis – and don't forget: cash on delivery.'

She goes to get the – parcel? The envelope?

'I wonder if it's legal?' Tania says.

'It's bound to be, somewhere, where we go,' says Lia. 'Let's talk about the car. It's a Lotus – "Om..." and all that. I had it built from parts. The engine's special, but no one will notice us, I'm sure – there's lots around like us.'

Lia drives fast. I crouch down in the back, the bird's cage hangs above me, on a hook screwed in a pole. The hook's a question mark, the bird's another, just like Madam Feng had said.

'Can we trust Madame Feng?' asks Lia.

'Of course,' says Tania, 'she didn't charge him for his room. And I peeked in the parcel.'

I miss my mattress, the room full of futures. I wish I'd made myself over when I was 13, become a pirate, maybe.

Outside, there's many countries. Lia says, 'These places are full of Nazis. They had to go somewhere, and have kids. I don't go for all their *sadomaso* – I like my body, so does Tania. It goes to show what scallywags can do – with a state, and all those profs.'

'What's the news from Marcel's state?' I ask.

'Oh,' says Tania, 'it makes do with refugees. I shouldn't stereotype, I know, but people have to end up somewhere...'

'Egon sells the odds,' says Lia. 'You need to be a genius to sell them. They're just arithmetic. The state department makes some threat, and Egon calculates the odds – too much? too little? hit or miss? He's lucky to be over there – the Russians, they just do it. In China, they're used to gaming, they don't need consultants. I think they fix things anyway.'

'Lia!' shouts Tania. 'Hang a left! We're tipping off the corniche!'

The parcel's stashed beneath a seat. We're stopped by cops, one says, 'Your bird is lying down.'

'I know,' I say.

I know what's in the parcel too – it's only cash. Too little to pay off for some sparky action. It's to do nothing. A retainer, for retainers. That's all right, and means the order comes direct from Madame Feng, not from some government.

I get out the car: I say, 'My country doesn't issue passports. Not if you're critical, or have some secret that they think is theirs.'

The cops don't want to bother with me. 'Maybe you come from Mars,' one says, and laughs. We all laugh. There's a fragrance in the Lotus – summer meadows, geese with yellow eyes. Perfect peace. We are all in her debt, good Madame Feng, who knows how to fix a car.

'Let's liven things up,' I say, as we race off. 'Let's give the whole parcel to the next guy on the list. Tell him – "we're running". See what happens.'

'I know what happens,' Tania says. 'I read the reports. Right through.'

I want to go back to the hotel, the room that's full of everything, you just catch a tail, and pull, it's in your eyes, your mouth, your nose, yet all around is pristine. The walls like parchment, unwritten upon, the floor like packing paper – no address; the ceiling white as letters unwritten, unsent, unimagined. 'I don't do food,' said Madame Feng. 'But I can read you recipes.'

'We've done France,' says Lia. 'They don't sell gas unless you get the grammar right.'

'Lia!' says Tania sternly. 'We missed out on Africa because of stereotypes, your myth about the poor guys there. I'm sure there's poor guys here as well, so's it'll all make sense to you. You're an exaggerator, Lia, there's nothing more to say.'

'We're out of gas anyway,' says Lia. 'Grammar or no.'

'Try Austria,' I say. 'The language of Schubert. Remember, *"Fort mit unerfliehter Schnelle"* – the unwelcome speed, the waves bearing us away – the beautiful meadow where I once found her... Mrs Feng, no doubt... vanished. How apt it all is,' I say, weeping with nostalgia.

'No!' says Lia, 'we'll find the guy in Italy. Open the vase of tragedies...'

'And Russia next!' Tania says. 'My feet long for Petipa, I'll be the Sleeping Beauty. Oh, how I'll dance and charm you, make you forget what happens next.'

When you drive fast like this, there are no landscapes. You have to look more closely at what isn't there. 'I think Hugo would be satisfied,' I say. 'If there had been one bit of justice done down where he lives – instead of song and prayer.'

'Wars aren't known for making justice,' Lia says, accelerating.

'It wasn't a different world he wanted,' I say. 'It was to see the old one held to some account. People should try harder...'

'This is the Ticino,' Tania says. 'They're used to money parcels here.'

A professor-type comes up. A white moustache not going anywhere. He says, 'Hey, you guys – you, the spirits of the Lotus – well met.'

We give him the parcel, 'My,' he says. 'I didn't expect this much. Madame Feng – she always says, "there is no top, there's no beginning", and so, "no depths, no end", so "don't look for me in either place". Quite unpredictable, where she is.' He's pleased with himself: 'You know,' he says, 'there's fifty Africas. Each one transforms so rapidly – although, of course, some are still stuck. The sixteenth century, as we would call it.' He shakes his head.

Tania says, 'We had a friend who thought there was just one, one country there that would draw on the rest.'

'Oh no,' declares the prof, 'that's now quite wrong. Now, it's all different, and quite complicated.'

'Those Tuaregs...' says Lia, hoping to lead him on.

'All types of trade, all types of gangs,' he says. 'Religion's all around, of course, but not all that important. Cash is the thing. And work.'

I'd like to talk about the motel, and the flag. Instead I say – 'The parcel. What's its destiny?'

'Oh no,' he says, 'don't drag me in, not to all that.'

He's not about to tell. 'Look at those mountains, those are exactly where the Frankensteins hung out,' he says.

We don't look up.

The guy trots off. 'Now what, Lia?' Tania asks. 'Everyone we didn't pay will spot us – this goddam car, Lia – you have to drive what grabs the eye! An obsession!'

'What else is there, Tania?' Lia asks. 'I believe in it, being seen. Do you believe in something?'

'We can't go back to Madame Feng,' I say. 'We disobeyed. We were unjust. Although – I miss that room, the mattress – that space to fill, or not...'

'We've got no cash,' says Tania. 'Why did you give it all away? The goddam parcel, all of it!'

I hadn't thought. 'It just seemed easier that way,' I say.

'Come on, *maestro*,' Lia says to me. 'Speak. Do. Resolve.'

'OK,' I say. 'Dump the car in that escarpment. Hitch a ride down to the sea, work our passage to Africa. Have Hugo – or Marcel! – have some guys ferry us down...down to the new State. Real Life... True communism. The critical. Adorno – no commodification, and no fetishes. No jargon, nothing improvised...'

I would go on, but Lia and Tania stare at me. 'No, no,' they say. 'Something deep. We should explore the fundamentals. Why do we switch from sex to Eros? What is a life? That kind of thing.'

'Be content,' I say. 'The mystery of life's a mystery. Dump the car and see if it will burn.'

Tania hunches over. 'It's the end of the road,' she says. 'And whatever we do, the future isn't going to change. It never changes, it waits for us.'

'Come on, Tania,' Lia says, like she's in an adventure tale. 'You have to suffer lots before you want to be a martyr. I'm not tough enough for that – so figure if you are! And don't say how the past is always changing – mine isn't, it's fixed and on the book.'

'Quiet, you two,' I say. 'We have to torch the car – that way we go back, back to Mrs Feng, and say the money burned.'

They say that Madame Feng's indifferent, and if the cash went to the Tuaregs, well, good for them. 'I'm sure it was some charity stunt,' says Tania. Maybe she's right.

We leave the burned-out car, the bird is in my pocket, quiet, and probably content.

I go back to Madame Feng, and tell my lies: she says, 'My little red friend? I loved to see him dance.'

'Tania dances too,' I say.

'You should leave them to it, your friends. You'll find your emptiness for sure; in the city, in the meadow, in the forest. Where's of no account,' she says.

'Where was all the money going, Madame Feng?' I ask.

'Oh, the usual things – humanitarian,' she says.

'Where was it from, Mrs Feng?' I ask.

'Oh – I guess it came from them who needed it, and back – quite roundabout. Not from the bottom ones, of course.' She searches for the key to my room. It's quite empty, but locking it – makes you feel secure.

'The guys you didn't pay – they'll be round soon,' she says. 'But first they'll do their sums with who you gave it to. The cash.'

I don't bother with more tales. The fault was Tania's.

'They'll send the soldiers in to Marcel's place,' says Madame Feng. 'That flag is a disgrace, a provocation.'

'It's transit, Madame Feng. You buy stuff there, and set out on the road. It's not a city you can smash,' I say.

'That's sentiment,' she says. 'You can't calculate the odds that way. Dignity, respect – how'd you slip them in your mix? In the end, the only destiny is martyrdom. Will you deny that to a guy?'

'I know the money comes from football, Madame Feng,' I say. 'In some way. In Harbin I dare say you paid a lot so they could play...'

'From football, into football,' says Madame Feng, like it was a manifesto. 'In Harbin, we Russians managed everything – the dentists, theatre, and dance. Mister Feng, of course, was Manchu. That makes all the difference...'

'Yes, I guess,' I say. We each have our tale to tell. 'They say kicking those balls – it gives you peace inside. A national team from Azawad... why not? Me – just of one thing, I want to make some sense. Hugo, the animals. The Tuaregs – what'll become of us.'

'No, no,' says Madame Feng, easing a tear to slide along her whiskery cheek. 'That way, my dear, you'll never end. You need to start with a resource, then spread it round, and watch it all come back – but multiplied.'

'The cash,' I say. 'Can that come back?'

'It better had,' she says.

Tiring of this, Madame Feng says, 'As for sense, what there is, is in the thing itself. You want something more; that, you must add. That way, you can understand

everything, but it's a meaning only to you.. Think of my
trafficking that way... I'd have you work for me, but
coming down to it, you can't do anything much at all.'

All is resolved – the usual unsatisfactory way. Tania
hunches by the wall again: 'Is this my fate?' she croaks,
'Reading maps? They mean that someone else has gone
before, and trodden out the new, as if it was a grape. The
maps – do they give a glimpse of where I want to be?
One-dimensional. A tragedy,' and she laments. I say,

'Tania, you have no destiny. Sit back and watch the
play. It ends, like you, and then the players go outside,
become quite other beings, you'd not recognise. You
make the drama...' and she interrupts, 'You cretin! That's
not how plays are done. They're written down, rehearsed.
Everybody follows orders – down where Hugo lived,
what's happened was through people doing what they're
told. Some boss instructed them – "There is no happy
land, no sisterhood, no sitting in the park and watching
puppies with their rhinestone bibs. For you – it's work,
with little profit and no joy. And that's the best part –
most of you will have it tough, you're squeezed until your
juice runs out your eyes..."'

'Yes, yes,' I say. 'No revolution was betrayed. It all
turned out as someone wants.'

'At last!' she says, 'you've grasped it. But not
"someone wants". Reason and discipline: to save from
defeat and chaos. Hugo got the whole thing wrong –
there's no point in our visiting, wafting along towards
him, those accusations, those false hopes – that maniac,
that demon Lia, driving us among the lions... There's
nothing that will fill your emptiness. You think you've
made preparation for a harvesting, but into nothingness,

the purity, the laying waste, the state that's critical –
nothing at all will come...'

'I like it just the same,' I say, offended. Tania weeps.
The dance, the whirligigs, the air... melts into air.

'Look, Tania,' I say, 'I'm the one who's worked. I
keep things going, keep things clean, austere, and logical.
You – you're a slob. You've given up your job, your food.
Maybe you're in love, it's of no interest. I give you orders
– you don't follow them. I could enforce, I guess. What's
the point, of an analysis without a point? And Lia,
smashing up the cars, racing when there's no one there...'

She looks at me, her face, emptying of tears, a red
balloon deflating: 'That's crap,' she says. 'What you want
is always changing. What you think – every moment,
something new crosses that white space.'

Lia and Tania – they doss down in Madame Feng's
salon. There is the samovar, a gold World Cup, and
souvenirs – gods of all powers, churches in snowstorm
balls, dolls – in those tiny bowler hats, the saris, the dish-
dash well represented here – and scores, in manuscript,
there's Tristan, Robert the Devil, Penelope... 'Some are
sweet memories,' says Madame Feng, straightening a
cossack's hat, his silver pistols and his mannequin's face
quite black and venerable. 'Most are bad debts. That
world – it's all quite gone. The travelling, the drinks at
sunset, the philosophy at dawn, watching the ibis pick its
way through broken amphoras... You'd only get that joy
nowadays by driving trucks. Give you more time to think.
The countries... ah! the countries, all gone under,
smashed....' Yes, here's a *fascio* of old banners, 'unite'
some say, a pot of folded peacocks' tails, deflated balls
and studded boots.

'This is real treasure, Madame Feng,' I say. 'You'd need a desert to lay this out in splendour.'

'Oh no,' she says, 'that's where it comes from. See how flat it is, how scrubby, sandy, undulant – some footprints last a thousand years – but mine, my dear... my body's light as tumbleweed, the valuables, they blow away, they drift, they end up here, my own, my little caravanserai, just footprints in the sand.'

A song comes in her head – I hope she doesn't croon, about the sand, the camels hobbling through. Or shrimpboats, as the sun goes down. 'You're absolutely *kitsch*,' I say, and 'Yes,' she says, 'but that's what drives the world. The state that Marcel founds, the future Egon cogitates, Lia's old motors, Tania's fears... The only way to do philosophy right now,' and she brightens, 'is drive a truck. And see the world.'

'There is my empty room,' I say. 'That's new and clean. Things could be put in.'

'I'm not so sure about the clean,' she says, 'and I can't drive. And you can't fill your room – with anything. That's why it's gratis, free, for now.'

I tell Lia what Madame Feng had said. 'Oh well,' she says, 'there's worse than *kitsch*. Everybody has the ideal of what they thought things ought to be. Look at back there – the happiness, the living free, the jolly slaves. It's different now. The flag design that Marcel stole – that's fairly naff – but there it floats. People say – "One day, that is the way that it will be", though what they mean is "long ago, one day, that's what we hoped it was". Things aren't so bad, remember, don't look back. Don't go in the toilets in the Empty Room – where Clara's son went in, and turned to art. That's not the worst thing either, but it's fairly definite.'

'What Madame Feng needs,' Lia says, 'is animals, about to be extinct. She puts them in the salon, so's they are preserved.'

'And then there's all her kids. She must have hatched a football team,' says Tania, 'and with reserves.'

I say, 'Madame Feng knows what she wants, and has it all collected here. The problem is – I tell you what to do, and you don't do it.'

'You're just another Hugo,' Tania says. 'What's done is all that can be done. The poor – they will be rich, the rich become the poor. Or maybe not. What more can you expect? Where Hugo lives, there is no civil war – and that's the best that they could do. It's sweet, you worry about what guys earn – it's all beyond you. Beyond them too.'

Later, I'm called in to the salon. Lia and Tania are drinking bourbon from a cup they share. The guy we gave the money to is there.

'Alphonse has apologised for you,' says Madame Feng, sour as a lime. 'The money has come back, and multiplied, just as I said it would.'

Alphonse looks unhappy. 'Cleaning – starts at the top,' says Madame Feng. 'A revolutionary principle. Alphonse will take this junk. All of it. The cossack's horse...' Alphonse wriggles. 'And all the floors beneath, that you can't see, will never visit, and are full of stuff – he'll clear. You wanted to know what life's about – well, it is this. Emptying. And death as well.'

The horse is on wheels, Alphonse pushes it towards the window – we don't help. 'The guys he owes – they'll all be after him, and whatever of these souvenirs was nicked – he'll have the owners on his back,' says Mrs Feng. 'That leaves me free, and unencumbered. For you three – here, there's nothing left. Unless you'd like... a memento. Death, though, is always in your eyes and at your back. A gewgaw doesn't help.'

Lia looks as if she'd like to take the golden cup, a peacock, the fountain where the fighting fish go wrassling... 'No, no,' says Tania. 'Nothing, thank you Madame Feng. Your children might deserve a thought...'

'No, no,' says Madame Feng. 'I spare them that, the darling girls, wherever they have gone.'

She pushes us roughly from the hotel. 'You,' she says, thumping me and toppling me down the steps, 'are a shell already. You two,' pulling Lia and Tania after me, 'will start off, new all over. Luckier than those two old woodlice in their log, Marcel and Egon – founder of states, and dicer of the universe. Bonaparte and Heisenberg – massacre leaning on the arm of happenstance.'

'I don't feel a bit different,' Tania says, 'though I might like to.'

'That's the good part, Tania,' says Madame Feng. 'Enjoy it.'

'Can I still drive?' asks Lia, rather naive and scared, 'if we're all new?'

'Oh yes,' says Madame Feng. 'It's like the bicycle. You might fall off, but you don't forget the how.'

There's Alphonse, and his flatbed truck. 'All *kitsch*,' he says, 'the past.' He is in overload. He seems morose. 'Remember,' he says, 'they're after you as well.'

'I'll always have a motor,' Lia says, as we walk down the path. 'I win, and so it's free. It's fixed.'

There's something flashing overhead. 'It's Madame Feng,' says Tania. 'Her rings. It's Cyrillic Morse – "see you again", it says. Or – it could be Chinese...'

'*There* was a woman,' I say. 'Packed full of meanings. Like an egg. A Fabergé.'

'The money, the football,' Tania says. 'I thought football was a metaphor – but it was all just cash, and kicking it around – knowing who you give it to, not where it ends up, having reproduced...'

'Changing the rules of any game – it costs,' says Lia wisely, jumping in an open car, delivered for us, new.

'It's an Isotta Fraschini,' she says, 'but up to date...' and on we drive. 'The sea...' she says. 'It doesn't look a bit like wheat...'

'Lia!' shouts Tania. 'Stop this nonsense, mind the cliff... and now! Block the road.'

Lia blocks the road. Some grey-green vehicles draw up. 'I'm sure they're military,' Tania says. 'They must be going to the front. They're off to fight the Russians.'

'No, Tania,' Lia says. 'They're made of plywood. They're Potemkin tanks.'

'Absolutely that's not so,' says Tania. Maybe she saw it in the future – that they were tanks, did make it to the front – or that they weren't, did not.

'We have to stop these guys,' Tania says. 'Be for the Russians – for sure, they'll have another revolution, much better than the first. They alone – they have the knack, you see it in their eyes. My folks are there, that's how I know. It's brewing up. It's not the war I mind, there's lots to come, it doesn't pay to be a squeamish type. No – it's that particular destiny... leave them alone to do it, they'll know how...'

'Well, Tania,' Lia says, trying to start the car. 'You've stopped them. I guess their shift is up. They're backing off, the soldiers, away to narrow beds. They're quiet for now. We have to trust your memory – though it's not clear, if you stopped the future, or just went along with it...'

'Oh, Lia,' Tania shouts, exalted. 'Who cares? It's done. I did it.'

Maybe it's all true. It's a great thing to have done. Hugo would be proud, I guess.

We sleep well in the Isotta. When we wake, we're on the ground, there's nothing left, except an 'X' of rust upon the asphalt, two bulbous shining eyes, a slick.

'It rusted out,' says Lia. 'How people love old cars – they are dream cars, and I dreamt, yes, how! – but I shan't tell.'

There's no sign of the grey vehicles. Perhaps they've already forgotten.

'They'll have been going to Africa,' says Lia. 'The guys here are humanists. They go where they can. There's ships, right over there...'

'You should have given more orders,' Tania says to me. 'Everyone else acted in period and in character. You just think of that fucking bird, and wait.'

'You did well, Tania,' I say. 'No one could do better, even if results were, well, from ambiguous to poor.'

'I told you,' she says. 'I'm not a humanist. I don't do stops and starts. You can't change time. Remember what they say, the thing is not to change the world, but understand it.'

'That's what Madame Feng believes,' says Lia. 'I understand it all quite well. Now, I'm without my wheels. I guess I'll have to run, rely on legs.'

'Alphonse says he'll have us work for him,' I say. 'We're not welcome back in Madame Feng's hotel, though she has empty rooms. If we're with Alphonse, there's lots of guys that work with us who'd like to see us dead, and take a hand in it as well...'

'How is the future, Tania?' Lia asks. 'We need to know before we seek an ally.'

'Oh,' says Tania. 'Bad. It's very bad. I am not there. I don't think it could be worse.'

'Whatever the catastrophe,' says Lia, 'there's always somewhere good remains. Or maybe not good – but not so bad. The thing's to find it.'

'We're very close,' says Tania, 'we three. So close, we should watch each other, every move. It would be betrayal, if someone found a refuge, went off, didn't tell the rest. Punished accordingly.'

'Hugo wanted to make a place that's good, a shelter for a whole population,' I say, expecting their derision.

'Hugo was a tyrant about happiness,' Tania says. 'I'm sure he's dead by now.'

'I have a problem with what Hugo talked about,' I say. 'Capitalism. And – The Other. The Alternative. What – when neither works? Both have grinding mechanisms... practice, logic. We're not humanists – we don't specify what works, nor what that "works" might mean...'

'Listen,' Tania says. 'You haven't made your mind up. You don't stand anywhere. Standing's not an answer anyway. Hugo wanted to leave something when he went, he died; some part of him. You don't. You just don't want to go. You know there's nothing that is left, when you're not here. Me? I wouldn't be bored, by my immortality. I quite look forward to it. I would make sense of all those dead, give them a hook to hang on, tags on bags of bones.' She does a step or two. 'What a waste, we were young and all that went to dust as well...'

'We must get moving,' Lia says. 'While you talk on, the minutes burn away. You don't have time. There's so much of it, but it has no trace, no substance. Just leaves dead things and losers, nothing of itself, you can't recall it, stop it coming, see it, eat it...'

'Your best time – it's the shortest, Lia,' Tania says. 'Take the least time – and you've won your race.'

'Alphonse says – work for him – or it's the cops,' says Lia.

'It sounds a good choice,' I say. 'Alphonse's work – the humanitarian round – it's not real hard, but puts us on the toilers' side. And on the other hand, that "working for the cops" – it shouldn't take much skill...'

'No, no,' says Lia. 'Alphonse could get us put in jail. He means that kind of cop, the punishers.'

'Then we'll sign up with him,' I say. 'How shall we present ourselves?'

'We'll have to take the train. Or the Métro,' Lia says. 'You could run us, me and Tania. You – the pimp. No sex. It's a good disguise, no one will touch you. Just look as if you know the trade.'

'It sounds too easy to be true,' I say.

'That's not what I want,' says Tania. 'Anyone can pretend to be a tart. I want to dance in feathers. Every night – just feathers, at the Red Mill, where everyone who can would want to dance. There, they have the skill to make those uniforms: – just feathers. No cache-sexe, and no sex.'

'A *poule de luxe*, Tania!' Lia says. 'That's what you'd be. But – twice a night, Tania, kicking and strutting in your plumage! Now, how'll we do our traffic? A man, with two women, on the subway – there's a message unequivocal. The guy's a pimp. No kidding. A cover perfect – better than feathers, that's for sure.'

'If we're to be successful criminals,' says Tania, 'I don't see why we have to play the hetero game – if that's what us pretending to be prostitutes involves.'

'I never said we'd be *successful* criminals,' I say. 'Just for security, and making cash. It's not success we'll get, just failure we'll avoid.'

'You needn't enter deeply in the game, you know,' says Lia. 'It's not a thing you win or lose in, Tania.'

'Exactly!' Tania says. 'If there's no winning in the game, it's not a game.'

'They'll kill us if we don't,' I say. 'It's not Cambodia – we have a chance of coming out alive.'

'We're alive now,' says Tania. 'Need we go through all this?'

'Madame Feng – she is behind it all,' I say. 'She thinks in stereotypes. I want to go to Africa, not act a role.'

'I don't mind acting,' Tania says, 'but this part's pretending to be in another part.'

'Quite classic,' Lia says. 'It reveals, like taking off the onion's skin reveals it's just an onion underneath. Besides – I'm the loser here. I was on top, a racer, till I found you in the Empty Room.'

'That's classic too,' I say. 'To blame the drink.'

'What we do goes in our skin, and stays for ever,' Tania says.

*

Egon and Marcel – hey! They remember us. 'Look out!' says Egon's message. 'If Lia came from Guadelope, a violent place, she's fine in France – if Guatemala, where the Yankee stooges killed those millions, she's got no papers. You and Tania – who knows where you come from – there is no proof, no proof either for where you want to go...' And Marcel adds, 'I have a country waiting for you – the passports very reasonable. There is no capital – but if you want to stay, it's capital you must bring and leave to fester there...' and he talks of the mud palaces, the pink birds rising from pink water, the markets where there's everyone for sale. All stereotypes. 'There is a death, too, they want to hang around your necks...' he says.

'The drink has got to them,' says Tania.

'No, no, it's the child you killed,' I say. 'The chicken. Tania's ghost.'

'It's cars kill people,' Lia says, 'not me. And don't you know – all chickens end up dead. Think on that, dear Tania. Better a live *horizontale* than one stretched out in its box. Or in its pot. But Tania – I could eat you, roast you, every slice... The aesthetics doesn't bother me too much.'

The two are sitting in the métro, I stand over them. Other people sit and stare at us. It could be an old French movie, with a moral. The passengers could have lives more interesting than ours.

'Lia,' I say, 'are you looking for forgiveness? Revenge? Redemption?'

'No, none of those,' she says, looking puzzled. 'We shouldn't be in this kind of transport, that is all. Isn't it anomalous, that we should look like prostitutes, try to convince these guys who don't seem interested?'

'You never know who's looking for you, who is after you,' I say. 'It's the cover, that's what counts.'

In my head, I make the movie – at least, a treatment and the stills for the publicity. The moral aspect's compromised – our cover story – and yet it is the scaffolding. Maybe bring in some myth? We can't afford to do it in boutiques – we'll set it in the street. They finish with a death – I must make sure it isn't mine. The director's voice – is not quite "he" and not quite "I". To put philosophy in deep – it's all ceramics, meaning nothing as you hang them on the wall, they enter in the owner, leave the maker far behind... maybe a dog could be the key, it runs out, you follow, if you're interested, then you search, then there unfolds the crucial time you're running after it. The crucial time. Time is what fill us out, immaterial: making our finitude.

'Let's get off now,' says Tania. 'No,' I say, 'we can go there and back again. We have to meet a guy at Clignancourt...' Some guys in uniform get on. Two of us – we have no papers. They want to see our tickets, though I've never seen this done before. We have two tickets between three. We pass them round. We're free. Undetected too.

We collect the humanitarian parcel. The guy says, 'It will spread goodness everywhere. The shame is – goodness should come from the thing itself, not the cash you spread on it.' We three agree, eager to get away. I hear him say to Tania, pointing at me, 'You've no need to have that gloomy guy running you two beauties...'

They still use the siren when the train's about to leave. If I were a composer, it would appear quite often, howl like Elektra.

I say to Lia, 'The guys here – the ancient ones look like commissars of police, the younger ones like hoods. I

wonder if this disguise of ours doesn't attract attention –
maybe it's a bad idea to go around like this...'

Lia says, 'We could just walk away. Start up the
same thing on our own. Go back to the bar. Save people.
But we won't. We three – we are a hive, a cell, point of
resistance – larvae, a bud, a shoot. We – we are bread.'

I hesitate. Then, 'I can't go all the way with that,' I
say, 'Lia, there's friends, of course, and then there are
one's plans.'

'It's just me and Tania, then,' says Lia, briskly. 'And
you with Madame Feng, and Alphonse.'

We loiter on the platform. What are we carrying?
'Military secrets,' says Tania. 'That's what they call them.
They don't work if they really are occult and don't go
bang.'

'Diamond rings,' says Lia. 'Like Madame Feng's.
Given out in Africa, for every confinement.'

'It's all philanthropy,' I say.

Elektra screams. An old guy stares at us, and Lia
goes behind, to push him on the tracks. Yes, this is the
movie that I want – spying on spies, the good – maybe the
bad – triumphant in the final take. Lia's too late, her thrust
just pushes him inside the car: he turns, '*Pute de putes,*'
he says.

We take the next train, 'This goes to parts of Africa,'
Tania says. 'You can be content with that.'

There's two guys, in alpaca outfits, come to mingle
with us ordinary folks. One says,

'I'll send the army to Africa. I would recruit the
world, put everyone in boots. Stability – that's what
they'll bring. Then they come home. The soldiers follow
orders, when there are none, they're a bunch of thugs –
like these around,' he gestures us all in. His comrade says,

'Lots of the troublesome ones – they're already military.'

'Lots aren't,' says the boss: I crane over to hear the word – 'Tuareg'. I lean in too far. 'Hey,' he says. 'You spying on me?'

'Pute de putes,' says the other. 'You pimp!'

The disguise is good. It works.

'I've grown a lot,' says Lia. 'Riding the trains here, aimlessly.'

'Oh, 'says Tania, 'for sure we'll be written up in history. There's no sex here, people will fill that in. But our story – it's a classic. Me – I've developed too, from knowing about time, things happening – to not caring, and not knowing.'

'I have more to give,' Lia says. 'Beyond assassinations casual. Something explosive. I have campaigns, I know what is the right, I have my grievance.'

'Mister Alphonse won't agree,' I say, 'to deviance.'

'He's not a real professor,' Lia says. 'It's what they call the mad guy, the boss who reads a newspaper in the jail. Real profs – they don't read them.'

'Let's take advantage,' Tania says. 'The traditions... Let's go see some rappers, painters, bareback riders – not scum like what we work for.'

'Yes!' says Lia. 'A writer, with bare feet, ring through her nose, and parquet floors and afghans on a string...'

I do it. A writer's found. I pay to fix a date: the writer turns me in. I pass the parcel – Tania takes and hides it.

'The finger of suspicion...' says the cop – or maybe he's a soldier too.

I say, 'Stability – you guys want that. Leisure and luxury as well.'

'Yes, yes,' he says. 'If life were not all stereotypes, where should we be? Begging in tunnels, that's for sure. But – there's reason and revolution too. Don't forget that.'

'Oh,' I say. 'Absolutely not, I don't forget. Our interest in the Tuareg,' I say, forestalling him, 'is ethnological.'

'No, no,' he says, 'the prof, Alphonse – he has us fish you in. We check his philanthropic work. But – you are clean, I see...'

He lets me go, thrown back into the pool. I say to Tania, Lia, 'Maybe we should seek another kind of trade. Here, everything is known, discounted...'

'Madame Feng, Alphonse – they are transparent. They cut a path through life. We aren't like that. With us, it's fog, meanders,' Tania says.

'Yes,' says Lia, 'I've quite lost reaction. I think it was that talk of love – they think you use it as a fuel, but I've no idea at all of where you pour it, and do you steer.'

We stand and watch a bird, a budgerigar – pick cards from a tiny pack. 'It's kind of begging,' Tania says. 'The guy who runs it lacks respect, I'm sure. And yet – it's just about the cleverest thing I ever saw, it turns your universe. It isn't magic, that bedraggled thing – it's science, reason...'

'I read a book about it,' Lia says, though she's impressed. 'The title was *Nonlinear Optics*. And yet – you'd swear there's no illusion,' and she shouts, 'Hey, birdie! The jack of diamonds – hard card to find!' and there! the budgie picks it out, and waits for more requests.

'I saw another like it,' Tania says. 'In Kiev. That shows there is conformity to one scientific law – repeatability.'

We stand and watch enthralled. 'Your bird – couldn't begin to work like that,' says Lia.

'No,' I say.

I think a while. 'It's not so brilliant, a budgie working for that tawdry guy, your life dwindling on the sidewalk.'

'There's your cop-out!' Lia says. 'You're quite the master of it.'

'What an unfortunate talent that bird has,' Tania says. 'It must long for resting in its cage.'

'They've sent the army, all over, to sort the Tuaregs out,' says Lia. 'And – did you see, the Russian and the French flag – they're just the same, a colour jigged a bit, that's all. It reminds me of the bird – he's a mystery recurring, picking and I guess – just sometimes missing – the right one, the card.'

'No one could miss the mauve flag Marcel stole,' I say. 'That reminds me of the cash – we know it came from dodgy things – the question is, where does it end up? Or, since cash never ends – where does its journey lead?'

The two aren't interested. 'We could go to Madame Feng's,' says Tania, 'but she doesn't live in places, she is just a tourist. That hotel chain she owns – the money's in the property, not renting rooms for guys to doss in for a night.'

'My!' says Lia, 'how you do talk on! I want adventure, preferably on wheels – camels or skates would do as well,' and she cartwheels down the sidewalk.

'Lia's quite a pain,' Tania whispers, 'and we never can decide who's to be Tristan...'

'Of course, you need to know these things,' I say, 'like – Madame Feng, changing the rules of football – she needs to tell the world... It makes up the global panorama, what they call the human cost, the skins on wires, all drying out.'

'At least let's enjoy the scene,' shouts Lia. 'Let me try the absinthe that's in those picture galleries, set before some bowler-hatted guy, morose as Dumbo.'

We sit her down. They bring a flask. 'It's green,' I say, 'to tell you it's a poison.'

'Nile green is my colour,' Lia says, drinking down and making faces.

'I'll pour,' I say. 'That is my thing.'

The sun sets behind the Tower. 'It's like a black lace jabot on a burning heart,' says Lia, hamming it, and slurring heavily.

We wait until she also sets, Lia's burning heart extinguishing. Her clothes, her face – they are grey-green, a military shade.

'Let's put her on a truck,' says Tania, keen to see a story worming out. We see trucks full of squaddies, off to Africa.

Tania says, 'The French guys always had it in for Tuaregs. Now is their chance to bring stability and shoot a lot of them. Lia will see it all, and maybe she'll go on, down to the south – taking her hangover to the Real Life state, a wakeup in Marcel's Motel – the Beau Geste – a fine tribute that,' and on she talks, stowing away poor Lia's arms and legs, while soldiers haul the rest of her inside the truck. She is a colour match to them. Nile green. They're quite morose, their helmets, as they drive away, could be mistook for topees.

'Love is a pain,' says Tania, 'and I hope they give
Lia desert boots... those burning sands...Yes, it's a pain,
that's why guys read about it, watch the movie, as the hurt
can't be located, though it can be cured. You know, Clara
has a rehab centre – kind of safari huts. The lions and
stuff poke their heads in, look at you – they say it turns
you off the booze.'

'Tania, you're upset,' I say. 'But what if Lia asks you
for a token – of your love, even expired... a slice of fresh
young liver? Yours? Plumping out the coked-up stump
she's left...'

'No, no,' says Tania, 'when romance is done – it's
like the setting sun. It's finished. Sunrise – it's a new orb.
The universe is full of them. No parting gifts.'

'We could go to cinemas together, Tania,' I say.
'Watch four programmes a day. No one will look for us.
We're just flies on a meniscus. Only drifters, larvae types,
sit and watch the water and the hungry fish beneath. We
are alone.'

'Yes,' says Tania, 'that is what I want. That is what
remains of love. Standing on the surface, watching the
flabby gasping creatures live their lives beneath. If I can't
dance, I'd wear my feathers, fly away.'

'No, Tania,' I say, 'sit with me. You can't dance, nor
fly. We have to wait for Lia. Just watch the stories. Sleep.
Hold my hand. Closer than that, in our two bodies, we
can't get.'

Closer than that, I don't want to be.

'If you're in a country,' Tania says, 'you must share
its suffering. Not now – way back, the past, the Indians,
provoked, exterminated.'

'Yes, yes,' I say. 'We know all that. Look! Delon.
Deneuve. Gabin. The monsters! Into the dark we go!'

Sometimes the film is thin and gossamy, you see right through, to the backing underneath. 'Don't snivel, Tania,' I say, 'Look – Jean Marais – wouldn't you like to be him?'

'Well, yes, I would,' she says, and brightens. 'But – *Beauty and the Beast* – we've seen it every day this week.'

'Lia will return,' I say, 'with news of Tuaregs, of battles, religion, devastation, peace. You must be patient.'

It's exciting. It's dark. I put my arm round Tania, pretend I'm someone else. 'It's *Zéro de conduite* again,' I say.

'Danger!' Tania shouts. 'There's guys in macs that's just come in the cinema!'

'No, no, we saw that one yesterday,' I say, but she is right, we're under threat. 'Quick!' I say, 'through the meniscus, through the film...' and hand in hand, we leap the rows of seats like hurdlers, headfirst through the screen, the pasty faces, the old suits, scatter the ranks of truckle beds... I think –

'Nothing. There is no dimension, nothing.' We are in the street. Safe but disillusioned.

'There was no thickness,' Tania says. 'No substance: it could be what we thought we saw, or Badlands. It's all without the thinness of a skin.'

The guys in macs don't follow us – maybe they're waiting for their money back.

'We should wait here,' I say. 'Lia will tell us about the justice done – to good guys, to the innocent, and bad guys too.'

We don't wait long. It's Lia! See, she limps towards us –

'You dull guys!' Lia says. 'I'd an adventure!' Her face is a grey-green.

'My dear!' says Tania, insincere. 'What lovely boots! And did you see some landscapes?'

'No, no, none of that,' says Lia. 'It was all pack and unpack, on and off the truck, and keep the lads' hands off my uniform.'

'Yes – but the motel? Clara's rehab unit? The religion? And the arms, the drugs?' I ask.

'They were all there,' says Lia. 'You've seen it on the screen. The Nazis in the Foreign Legion, burning sands. All that.'

'It seems to me,' says Tania. 'What they need down there is a Napoleon.'

She laughs, punches my arm, pretends to salute me.

'It all sounds rather vague,' I say. 'But for that I'd need a horse, a white one.'

'Oh,' says Lia. 'The army has a squad of those.'

'And did you win?' asks Tania. 'You look awful, Lia, just as though you did.'

'You'll know who is the enemy,' says Lia, whispering. 'As it's the ones who shoot at you. Unless it is your friends, in liquor.'

'Just tell us, which side were you on,' I say.

'That little state – Marcel's, it lives by trade,' she says. 'Everywhere could be like that. The poor people just move on, there are no jails – who wants to pay for idle guys?'

'The Tuaregs! Come on, Lia! Tell!' Tania shouts.

'Oh,' says Lia. 'How I envied them. They had fast wheels. If they promise to be good and love stability – we'll put them all in uniform, and on our side. The lads, in the truck with me, that's what they said.'

'That's not much of an ending, Lia,' Tania says.

'Don't be disappointed,' Lia says. 'When I was drying out, they tied me to a cot – an "X" I made. It's hard to trust anyone, when you're pinned out, an "X". I didn't want a cure. All I wanted was myself. Not victory – survival on my terms.'

'It's not clear,' says Tania, struggling to find some sense.

'Then – I come back here, and find you two, in the stalls, asleep in each other's arms,' says Lia. 'Two magpies, seeking the glitter. Want everything different, but always growing. Brighter, too.'

'That's what movies give,' I say. 'The taste for sparkle.'

'It's real combat down there,' Lia says. 'How do you expect it to end?'

'Don't worry about me, Lia,' Tania says. 'And our love. It was only movies.' They stand close together. Mrs Feng would say what people want is harmony, tough and granitic, and to get it, they suffer and submit, sometimes bite back and suffer much more. She's probably on the winning side. What if you're not? What if you don't want a victory, just things getting better all the time?

'Lia,' I say. 'I didn't put you on the truck. In any case, there's nothing for us there, down in the sand. It's not our stuff.' We contemplate: real combat... And for sure Lia didn't see them all, the Tuaregs – some scudding off in pickup trucks, others, most, squatted in tradition as it rubs away. It's indeterminate, and Hugo is no help at all. I say,

'Madame Feng told me, "It's not Confucius. It's just football. Remember – the more players on your side and on the pitch, the harder strategy becomes. What matters,

anyway, is the rules – the players come and go, they're all
for sale. The game is what there is, and all the game – is
rules."'

'Those guys down there – they're crazy, mad, angry.
To pull it all down and start again, from somewhere clean
and straight. That was me,' says Lia. 'I saw myself. I
understand them perfectly – though they're more
desperate than me. It's all a race. When you're ahead you
don't let on: you're cool. What do you win? Once, even a
season? It never is enough. Winning for ever, that's what
you want, and if some guy's ahead, you try to shunt them.
Although – when it's all done, you swear you're all best
friends. Maybe you are. The cash is good – it's therapy.
You spend it all on chocolate froth, and leave it in the sun
to melt away.'

'Your guys, those in the truck, the ones that didn't
look for Real Life, just wanted to kill mad dogs with
sticks – how did you feel for them?' asks Tania.

'The soldiers? They don't take sides. They're there to
see the fun. They like to watch the gladiators, identify
with them, think they're warriors too. They climb on and
off their trucks, in and out their trench... And all the
warriors die, even the punks...' says Lia, quite negative.

'Who tied you to the cot?' I ask.

'Oh,' Lia says, 'not the drink. I was angry mad. I
wanted combat. Mrs Feng – she wasn't mad, nor angry –
doesn't even know the words.'

'Lia,' Tania says, 'you're the only one trying to live
in nature. All the others – they plot, they scheme to have
tomorrow's bread. They have landscapes. All you desire
is seeing no one, no one ahead of you.'

'Banal and reactionary,' Lia says. 'That's all it turns out to be. I've given up. I'm not instructing you two lapdogs in what you could be doing.'

I say, '"Class and classification," Hugo said. That's all there is, while you're in the middle ground. It's like what you say, Lia. As for the rest – in the end is the beginning. The mud we came from, go to. Down to earth. You fly, and then you hit the mud.'

'Pretty and vapid,' Tania says. 'Beauty and the beastly, all in fun. It's a sutra. We can't go beyond ourselves; unless we make some super things, we'd look like pigs or cod, grown from twists of spit on dishes.'

'We don't know how, Tania,' Lia says. 'That's just fiddling anyway.'

I say, 'We still work for Alphonse, remember? Suppose we just drop out. Don't steal a thing, don't spy or snitch. Maybe that lets us out, to track on, going where we were.'

Lia and Tania, they make peace. They're quite miserable – they don't coincide.

We stop being criminals, and wait to see what happens to us.

On every corner, every bar, there's Alphonse, tracking us, a wireless to his ear – passing us on to other Alphonses.

Trucks go past – most full of Africans. Madame Feng is all around, she sends the cash to Africa, and back it comes, sometimes in human form. Sometimes she sends stability.

'Let's take a ride,' I say. 'Maybe the truck'll go down South, Lia will find some wheels, and off we'll go...'

'You didn't understand,' says Lia. 'Daytona. Then the Lotus. To win, you write the prayer, stash it inside each wheel. You win the race because the prayers revolve. You made us ditch the Lotus. The prayers ended, burned right there, pop-pop went the tires. Troubles began.'

'That's why I gave up the future, and the maths,' says Tania. 'To love my Lia. It was all disposed, until you sent it up in flames. Madame Feng, our inspiration...'

'I'm quite amazed,' I say. 'It wasn't at all like that. Emptiness means surely "nothing there". That's what she gave, she offered...'

'That's what you like to think,' says Lia. 'But it's quite clear, the opposite. Everything is always everywhere. The future too. As Tania knows.'

'That would be terrible,' I say. 'Nothing disappears? – not even in the toilets, where you'd think the Blanks would signify a vacuum.'

'No, no,' says Lia. 'Why, that's where Clara's son is now.'

'The suffering,' says Tania, 'it's all belonged to someone else, and we just pass it on when it has used us, our circuits, all our stuff.'

They're deep into it, the eternal crap. Surely the cinema could shake them out of their illusion, with its precious sheen of black and white...and grey: then rainbow, wraparound, and now reduced to midget-size... Always quite immaterial. Projected on every surface, wiped off without a stain. The proof of the ephemeral, all made by us, for lots of cash.

'Oh Lia,' I say. 'I'm so disappointed in you two. And Madame Feng, the great deceiver. No emptiness, just parcels, envelopes. And so – no beginning, no new start, nothing original.'

'Nothing has changed for us,' says Lia. 'I'm still furious. Beauty is still the beast. Nought for your conduct – that's what I aspire to.'

'Yes,' says Tania, addressing me. 'Forget what you feel uncertain of. You know it all, everything, already.'

'How's your bird?' Lia asks me.

'He's fine,' I say, patting my pocket. 'He's no flesh on him. The Mediterranean diet – that's the key.'

'I like a lean life too,' says Tania. 'There's no philosophy behind how I go on – bouncing off obstacles. You join in too much,' and she pokes me. 'Too many choices. You're a prisoner of those you didn't make as well as those you did. Living lean – it's not because it does you good, staves off catastrophe. It comes natural, and it works.'

'I've always been a disappointment,' I say. 'So I've escaped your complacency, Tania.'

We look to hop on a truck. Silent on the sidewalk, we wait for our ride. We lift up our eyes.

There's the big Tower, like Babylon's. It's not a great replica, doesn't get the idea... Made by some German guy, Herr Eiffel. The early cities were bigger, left more to pillage, absolutely razed. Beacons for ambitious people, looking for terrible places to bring in their terrible things – torn down.

There goes the American revolution – the one our non-founding fathers lived through – ending in songs.

'I can't believe it,' Lia says. 'We're really going to Africa, maybe.'

There's Alphonse, watching. I quite miss the Feng *pension*, her special philanthropy that faintly scents the air like ancient wax.

No violence has yet been done to us.

*

'Mind my knees!' shouts Tania, as we pull her up over the tailboard: 'Someone'll have to dance to get us bread.'

*

The guys on the truck – they're from every part of Africa. They won't go back. The chat is about football.

I say, 'You should be rich,' and tell them about Hugo. 'That's very long ago,' says someone. 'They try to save the birds right now. Some beasts have gone for good.'

'No,' says Lia, 'I was there. You stereotype, you guys. When the big war comes, you're better off down there.'

'Quiet, Lia!' Tania says, 'We'll keep it to ourselves.'

*

It's as good a place to start from, the one we left and now go back to. Thanks to the last envelope, we can go on board the early plane. Africa can wait. Back to New York, the Empty Room.

*

It's Egon, all fleshed out. 'Well,' he says, seeing I'm not thrilled to be here, nor with him: 'Here we all are, our old friends. Tania and Lia. You should have enjoyed sleeping with them...'

'Maybe I should,' I say, 'but not put like that.'

'There's lots of Syrians here,' he says, fishing for some talk. 'Lots of Iraqis – turned out to be Syrians. They hate it here.'

'No, Egon,' I say. 'It was Africa we were all to go to. And – your cosmology's all wrong, Egon. We never really left here, or only parts. A person's fairly much dispersed, parts left all over – where you came from, are going to, and are passing through. Some left with your parents – if you remember them. The strange passport that you carry. You swore on that.'

We look hard at each other: 'How's my Empty Room?' I ask.

'Condemned, it was,' he says. 'Health.' It would be that.

'Lia and Tania?' he asks.

'Lia went to Africa, and returned – now, she's in stasis, like Tania. Lia's into Buddhism. She's got no wheels. Tania's given up the future. I guess she's looking for someone to love. Be loved by.'

'I own a mass of Empty Rooms,' says Egon: he's clean shaven now, full of his news. 'It's a chain. They're all empty, some are buried. Under the sand – that's why they cost me almost nothing. Now, they're assets. The model – you won't believe! – there's a brasserie, modernist in style – the only one in the Sahel. That's the father of them all. So, no one's in them now...' He goes on, relentless.

'Well,' he says. 'You three. France. The country of the *noir* – the movie kind, not the people,' and he laughs. 'Trucking round the cash for hit men and guerrillas?'

'You're fishing, Egon,' I say. 'We looked for ways to start again. Emptiness. But that was an illusion. Everything in Paris got filled with plot, guys to run from, guys who give you rides. We're close now, we three, Egon, we're spiders, with our webs entangled...'

Egon's delighted – he's an owner, an entrepreneur. 'I realised,' he says, 'why I'm not a humanist. Our species is displaced. We are no longer central, not to anything. Not to ourselves, the universe, the new things we know. So – owning stuff. It fills you up. It's a something.'

'How about Marcel?' I ask.

'The dream,' says Egon, tickling his face where sideburns were, 'of every cop. A world without security. You don't need it, watch for it – just guys come in, they leave, they are no threat. Just guys. That was his state. Here – he's lost, of course. It makes him interesting – if you have the time.'

'Europe has the values, Egon,' I say. 'Lots of cash as well. Though – I and those two, the women – we didn't make the profit. What are we doing here?'

He's irritated: 'Empires – rising, falling, all around. Your Europa, gorged on blood, some bull's pizzle still stuck into her, twirling her pashmina... trilling to the new lads, the new expanders, who think "this time... it will all change". It will, but not so much,' he says. His anger grows: 'Maybe a little state? The Real Life one? That's specialised in selling things – lithium, maybe, or Mauritanians, or artificial guano? Or will you wait for it again – the big idea, like Hugo's? His future – there it stands, it works – always a step or two in front, always the bad signs, those black circling birds, the worms – red, yellow, grey. They're made to eat the corpses you accumulate,' he shouts. 'See! Tania's given up. She wants her Lia, or a person similar. Lia – runs ahead – but on measured tracks, quite circular. So,' and he grabs me, his new aggression flying in spitballs in my face. 'What do you want? Where do you go?'

'You've set it out for sure, the future, and the present too. I hoped to find a place to think it out...' I say.

'You guys, you questioners – you hunch over, like your little query sign,' he says. 'What can you see, like that? Always you're looking back. The question's in the past. The rest is blank. To be thought out...!'

'So, Egon, you'll just keep your chain of eateries, and watch them swell with worth?' I ask.

'I'm not into giving people work,' he says. 'When guys like you have got some, all they want is slacking off...' and on he talks. 'Hugo – he didn't stick by what they had agreed,' he says.

'Maybe he changed his mind,' I say. 'Found better reasons.'

'No,' Egon says. 'No doubt he always had his reservations. When he was quite alone – out they came, a swan song, in the wind.'

'Do you still look into the future, Egon?' I ask.

'Oh,' he says. 'I've still young guys around – they do that. The future costs too much to fix. That's why I'm into beverages.' Grudgingly, he asks, 'What'll you do now? And Tania? I've another woman now, of course. She depilates me.'

'I don't know much,' I say. 'I'm waiting for that gap...'

'Your parents – must have bought you something – some information?' he asks.

'Public school – public knowledge. Private school – private knowledge – that's what they said. I went to Greek school, briefly. They sent me there to learn about the Scythians – how they came from nowhere, riding hard, invisible; they cut you down – like scythes against the grass. You were dispatched. They disappeared without a whoop. There were fewer of you, and you felt defeated.'

'Your parents – they weren't Scythians?' he asks, suspicion in him.

'It was a thing we didn't talk about,' I say.

'I gave my helmet to Marcel,' Egon says. 'He needs a lift. He gave up his passport, for his little state. They don't have citizens, their passport's just a visa – fit for a transhumation. When they get a court, he's on a murder rap. The penalty is flaying. Nothing religious – it's a special hit, devised for Mr Big, whoever he is at the time. You see, the state is pure: in and for itself. If you mess up, it takes your inner self, and your skin is passed on to the next.'

'The barman wasn't Mister Big,' I say. 'Yet they think Marcel got his skin.'

'They wouldn't pin Marcel on that charge,' says Egon. 'A death is immaterial. The barman, though, was a big man in your bar. Perhaps he didn't have the big idea... Or else, it was so big we all had come to it before. No, I told you, Marcel's the founder of a state, his state. Geographically, it's small – but as idea, it's big as any one. If things go bad, he gets the blame – not for murder, for injustice. Marcel grew disillusioned with his job. And so, he made a state without security. It's in and for itself – I told you. No cops, no army. No subversion, and no spies. Just stuff to steal – so, no one blows up the warehouse, no one prays... Stealing stuff – it's just a redistribution.'

I feel I've somehow got involved.

*

My Empty Room, original, is sealed. I break the wax –
and there's the smell. It's life, like on brown strips, with
blobs of eager jello, blob on blob's shoulders, climbing up
the ladders, made of blobs. Here, there's bottles: in a
corner heaps of feathers, rusty brown. I turn them over,
maybe there is Tania underneath.

No.

It's really empty here. The toilets – sealed.

*

I said to Tania, before we left for the Sahara, 'It's nothing
much, the Real Life. Just a motel, now full, now empty,
always waiting for the next. Barely a state. No citizens.
The track in like the track out, identical.'

'No, I told you,' she said, 'it's everything. The
people, the families, now they flee and now they pray,
they traffic and they screw. See – they find refuge by the
motel. That, at least, if nothing more.'

'It's a flag on a line of huts,' I said. 'And you
complex guys, like Egon – you talk about the big idea and
what is wrong with this one or with that – but in the end,
you just want things improving for you, all the time until
you die. So – I don't go with this, the "everywhere is
everything". It's, well, it's empty.'

'You should see Egon's new woman,' Tania said.
'She's nearly everything.'

'There's billions that can keep you company,' I said.
'All related. It's just you who's found one that doesn't
suit.'

'Oh,' Tania said, 'this Francine – she doesn't speak,
she just designs. Moves furniture around, and paints the
walls.'

'Keep her out of my Empty Room,' I said.

'I've no doubt we'll shake the world,' said Tania, confidently. 'But Lia bothers me. So full of rancour... As for Marcel – Alphonse might go and watch the piles of merchandise. Keep us in touch with Madame Feng, and all her cash.'

*

We book an audience with Marcel. His arms are raised to greet, in general – there follows no embrace. There is no ring to kiss. I say, 'Madame Feng has rings – a surfeit too. And Mister Alphonse could mind the store...'

'Those crooks?' he shouts. 'They're worst of all. There's terrible trouble now – if I don't defend the citizens, I shall be flayed. There are no citizens. No One. No Body. Like Odysseus, the lying dog. Some wretched traveller, the nameless one – ends in my ditch, beaten and dead. Am I responsible?'

He's desperate. Lia bursts in – ignores the lifted arms. 'Yes!' she screams. 'You must be responsible! I'll be that traveller, the anonymous, the undocumented, the waif, the wisp, between genders, unprincipled, without a family, without insurance – ah!' she shouts. 'My wasted life! Suborned, pawed by that serpent,' and she scratches Tania's bland white face. 'Revenge! You pig!' and she spits at Marcel.

She races no more. She thinks the lover that she doesn't love, abandons her. We stand back, away from her. She's the wreck we've made, towering over us, the rockets armed.

Over there, that must be Francine. She is unmarked – no tattoos, no chemical colours on her face. 'Of course I talk,' she says. She must know that Tania says she's only interested in filling space. 'It's flatness I can't stand,' she says.

'You can't trust the communists,' Lia rants on. 'They want the biggest jobs. They tell you not to give to charity...'

'My family never gave to charity,' Francine says. 'I don't know if that means they were communists. I'm interested in dimensions, not in homes. I don't go home no more.'

'Don't be so stuck-up, pig!' Lia shouts at her, laughing at her own turn of words.

'The trouble is,' says Francine, ignoring her. 'With Egon. I'm a success. I'm not sure about him. And Marcel. If he's flayed – where would we put the skin? I don't believe in metaphor. A corner wouldn't do. Or painted blue, nailed to the front door?' and she smiles quizzically at us, a crooked smile, as if she's always smoked a pipe.

'If he's flayed,' says Lia, sharply. 'He wouldn't have a front door.'

'Well,' Francine says. 'You're all his friends, so you should know.'

'There's lots of micro states around,' says Tania. 'Marcel's is nothing special.'

'Those are on the edge, or hidey holes for rich guys,' Marcel says. 'Mine's central, and for working stiffs.'

Francine seems distressed. She says, 'I never saw such animals like you – I'm used to dealing with big city people – you all have some condition I've not seen.'

'The song says "Without God, everything is possible",' Tania says. 'We are possible as well as you, Francine.'

'I don't think it's a song,' I say, but Lia's humming it.

'It's "anything is possible", not "everything",' Marcel says.

'There's no difference, Marcel, and what it says, is true. You can't imagine...' Tania says. 'Though what will come's beyond imagining.'

'You said not to tell of that,' says Lia, calming down. She hugs Tania. 'There! You want emotion – have a bit of mine.'

'From you, Lia, it goes down crooked,' Tania says. 'I can't think why. They say emotion's good for everyone, like steak.' She turns on me: 'This guy, though, has no emotion. Just a plan he won't reveal.'

'Steak isn't good for where you got it from,' I say. 'Better a live plan than dead flesh any day.'

'That's cheap slogans from the seventies,' Francine says.

'Steaks come from beasts, not beauty,' Marcel says. 'And neither has to do with our emotions. Those are just sex.'

I must get away from these, who were my friends, and now have given up.

Egon bustles in, embraces his Francine, who slides away.

Talking to Francine – it's like talking football, with Mrs Feng. I must fulfil my plan, go down, close Hugo's eyes. I see him lying on a floor, they've stripped the place. Did they let the bird out? I ask myself, and there is no response.

'Look, Francine,' I say. 'You're a success, and so am I, we're complementary. You fill, I empty.'

'Oh,' she says. 'I couldn't come with you. But I could wait.'

'Then that would miss the point,' I say.

When the time came, I left alone, of course.

*

The plane goes down South. Out of the window, down there somewhere is Real Life, its little state.

I take a cab – and there is Hugo, exactly as I thought. On his back, the eyes open. Looking at the sky, the room pillaged, just like Babylon, with its stories of the first and last men. I wonder if there's a curse laid here. The bird – quiet in its cage. I lay it in my pocket, by my own. If Romeo hadn't met with Juliet – they'd maybe lie like this, silent, unknowing, unknown to one another.

Hugo wouldn't leave more written stuff. Everything was in his letter. There is no big book. No notes. If this is an observatory, there's no telescope to look through.

Everyone here, in the town and on the dusty roads, looks worried and content, like they do everywhere. Maybe it's not real life.

I close his eyes, like it's done in movies. It makes no odds to what he doesn't see.

A hotel – it should be Russian, or might be Chinese – I find one called the Harbin Hostelry. They haven't heard of Madame Feng, from Harbin. Egon's chain, his idle brasseries, is underground, of course. I go into a bar that's underground – there's nothing of Egon's there. I drink for Hugo, and for me, and Lia, Tania, and the rest. I ought to tell the Party Hugo's dead. I call a guy.

'I don't think Hugo stayed with us,' he says. 'We have no plan to honour him.'

Maybe I sound a little drunk. I'll call again. I found a tape, wedged in his floor. It's about the animals – a bird, a roaring sound, and chitter-chattering. Is that Hugo's bird? Whose speech is that? – animal or human... both?

I wonder – what is the ritual here? How do you bury? Hugo tried to sing that song – about the mallows. Or maybe they translate as hollyhocks, 'drifting away in the wind, gently, gently, servants of summer...' When he was drunk, in falsetto, he tried to sing the *Lied*. Who'd sing it now for him? It would seem incongruous – to dig a trench, to fill it with hollyhocks, cover him with flowers and hide it all again. Maybe – yellow convolvulus, and a vigorous march. Here, there are no hollyhocks, and he never had a servant, refused the idea of any tie subordinating. That includes mourners, I suppose. I think around all this, and then I dig. He achieved no real life, with a state, a flag. I wonder where the state is here... if it registers the deaths. I bundle up his rigid corpse and stuff it in a shallow pit.

That night, I lie where Hugo lay. Better would be an urn burial, in a pot with oily leaves. Or tar, to burn. Stuff him in. But he would break, not bend. Smoulder, not flame Then, there's the animals, searching the earth. The lower ones, all underground, undignified, a turbulent buffet... and there are dog-like ones who'd dig him up again, with their claws. Spread him out, then? Not his style at all. Think of the vultures. Was he a Zoroastrian? He would have left a clue. Maybe the bird... he, on the floor, the bird, all day looked down on him. A late conversion? – this place is full of Parsees. In the dusk, you see the birds circling the tall distant towers.

In the morning, the tomb is empty. It's a relief. I had my doubts – the colours, the animals, the nourishment, the putrefaction. A complex beginning I'd not thought through.

If you invent too much, you end with mausolea, Lenin's body saved forever in the dark ignorant Russian soul – you need to keep well clear of that. This way I've kept out of trouble, and I take the plane.

Some guy beside me says 'This place' – we're leaving it – 'It's like a parody – the US, when the slaves were freed. Look at them, down there, the banks, the mines, the skyscrapers, the presidents. And all those blacks, poor souls.'

I keep my counsel. 'I guess everywhere aspires to that,' I say. The guy goes on, 'Those US generals – they do their stuff. Then they cover up – but what they believe inside! If they die, they want to be decapitated, and their heads put in the fridge! Resurrection, Armageddon – that's the sane part. New Jerusalems, raze Babylon, put peoples into bondage – that's just the next step. My! They're so gullible – I guess they get it off the Net...' And he talks on.

When I'm back, Lia says, 'Did Hugo's Africa make some impression on you, then?'

'Well, you have to dodge the *mal d'Afrique,*' I say. 'And not exaggerate. Of course, there was the sunset, animals at night, the people walking up and down – all like we once did, like it is on the TV. I was there to bury – a humanitarian cause. Of course, I insisted with the Party, organised memorials, all that.'

'And were there clawmarks round the grave?' asks Egon. I hadn't looked.

'There was that stone age boy – buried naked in the sand, holding a blue stone – did you give Hugo his blue stone?' asks Tania. I hadn't thought of that.

'No message?' Lia asks, disappointed.

'Just the tape – domestic noises. What you'd hear around the shack,' I say. 'Incomprehensible. Hugo gave everything for the cause. You'd say his struggle was being right, and sticking to it.'

'We need someone knowing about Africa,' says Marcel. 'That's not Hugo.'

Marcel makes percentages from all the trade – I guess he knows what's needed. 'Don't forget,' he says to me. 'You owe me for the plane.'

'I don't think he'd have liked me,' says Francine.

'He didn't stand for liking,' I say. 'Hugo felt the continent was drifting, like a rotten tree, burning in the sun – guys picking wreckage from the sea and living under it, getting sick, and seasick, torturing and praying, trying to swim off, giving up – the thirst, the worms inside, black birds above... He wanted the wreck to be a ship, and everyone be sailors, going somewhere. He had a plan...'

It sounds banal. Illusory. I stop.

*

Lia doesn't know that if she took her beliefs more seriously, she should buy a cage full of common birds, down in the market, every month, and then release them.

The Flag

'Hugo was killed?' I ask Marcel. 'Who would believe it?'

'That's my character. I'd believe it. People do favours. Hugo had ideas people would avoid, and memories too. He had no backing – so the threat, him, could be removed without a fuss,' Marcel says. 'But – it might as well have been you who did it.'

'Why should I?' I ask.

'You said nothing. Made no report. And no one knows you, your motives, or their lack. We could try you, in Real Life. If you're innocent – good for you!' he says. 'Justice seen and done. That's the trick. It impresses, holds the attention. Always worth the while.'

'There's nobody,' I say.

'There's nobody everywhere, along with all the bodies,' he says. 'No one counts them. We all claim to be nobody, and not there, when it suits.'

Maybe the red bird is my proof – safe in my pocket... saw it all. The light, the death. As the song says, the living love the candle-flame, and hop right in. Hugo had nowhere else to go, nowhere was left.

'You've nothing, Marcel,' I say. 'There was nothing. Just space, bounded by bare walls, bars of a cage. Space – a disappointment, always relative. Some end of string always there, on the horizon.'

'Well then,' Marcel says, 'no trial, no extradition. We could use the Empty Room and all our skills to make a scenario of the future, the near past. Hugo would be in there somewhere.'

A hundred years ago – their characters would be worth a pause. Lia, Tania, their depths – intuited. Their families labelled and a-dangle from their tree. Their story, intertwined with love and panting – worth a memoir. I don't miss them, not at all, the last centuries – the story, the motives, the conformities.

I think of Mrs Feng and Alphonse, the Eiffel tower – a spindly thing with eateries – not the grand earthen cone, the tower of Babylon, now all cast down. Once, with every working stiff payrolled, his basket full of mud... up and down the ramps, until the Americans arrived, to knock it down...

'Your trouble is,' says Marcel, squeezing the muscle in my arm. 'You don't move on. Your ground is sterile. You're reactionary. I – we – are the Babylonians now. We take prisoners, but this time, we're smart – being king is not enough, so we do deals.'

'You do a deal about Real Life?' I ask, surprised, perhaps appalled. He doesn't answer. I shan't press him any further.

'Egon's chain,' says Marcel. 'Those bars. It's a necklace – sleeping pearls. A trade route, a road. Some day, someone will travel it, park their beasts, sing and sleep...'

'You'll never see it, Marcel,' I say. 'You'll be on a charge, or pegged out in the sand. You need an entrepreneur, an oligarch...' Then I see it, Marcel's future: 'Marcel! You have to marry Madame Feng!'

'I'm not the type,' says Marcel. 'You'd need a Ziggy, ready to do that for a spell, sequins... a show.'

'No, absolutely not,' I shout. 'She has the capital, and her simple soldier, Alphonse, who fixes everything. All you need, and more.'

'That's gross,' he says. 'I have my honour to consider.'

'You've got land, territory, Marcel,' I say. 'They'll kill you for it.'

'Look, my dear,' he says, unkindly, close to me. 'We know your childhood – worse than Ivan the Terrible's. And your ambitions – ever greater, and more changeable. For you, all is forgiven, nothing conceded. And – you're fascinated by Francine. She only wants to fill you up with furniture – when she's sure you're really empty.'

'She wants so little,' I say. 'It's a feat! Lia wants to win a race. Tania wants Lia. Those are big things, universes. But Francine... so little.'

'Don't be deceived,' Marcel says. 'She wants to shift her stuff, pile it on you, so she'll be a desert, then fill that up with something different. Meanwhile, she'll have submerged you with her decor.'

'Marcel – for you, Madame Feng's the answer. You'll come round to it,' I say. 'I see you – shaving slivers off cucumbers, making sandwiches with your wife, Good Madame Feng.'

'You've an odd idea of marriage,' Marcel says, though he's clearly tempted. 'Anyway, I'm now quite asexual. It happens to lots of soldiers. Alexander the Great...'

'Your integrity is lost,' I say. 'You didn't shoot the tsar and his little sisters – or didn't do it yourself. You know nothing of real life.'

'Our clients have to choose,' says Marcel, going straight again. 'They can have religion, or sell stuff – but not both. And as for you – no trial, no tsar. That is our bargain. Of course, I'm acquainted with Mrs Feng... her envelopes come in, then out goes trunkfuls, and the families multiply... quite exponential! Human capital!'

'It's all up to you,' I say. 'You do the deals.'

'The Tuareg,' he says, wincing. 'They have their boss – but they don't tell you who he is. Besides – the giants have gone. In college, I did Great Books. My only course. Then I dropped out – you can't add to those, the characters. You and I,' he hugs me. 'You are no holy fool. I – no Emma Flaubert. Then, when I was a marine, they said, 'Each of you's a gas bubble, a pustule in the liquid. You burst, you are absorbed – it isn't up to you.' Fichte. The individual in the nation – isn't worth a pop.'

'I can't imagine Hugo being offed,' I say. 'Although – you obeyed, you disobeyed – the scene was always terrible. There's no accounts no record. It's just oblivion. Death's caul lies tight on every face, the white, the black, the left, the right...'

'Oh yes,' he says. 'Where death's concerned – it is the long haul for us all. I'm thinking of decapitation. Freezing, waiting till they find a cure for our mortality. A line of former talking heads: no song, no dance, just like the birds. It suits. I'm now a head of state – so I'll remain a head, into eternity. One day, our tongues will thaw, as we're all lying side by side, we'll sing. But you won't hear us, my forgotten friend...' he puckers up, could laugh, or cry.

I think of Madame Feng, her ivory brooch, her precious rings; singing 'Kalinka', and 'The East Is Red' as she tips stained parquet planks down the chute from the top floors into the skip below. In her gift, the riches of all Russia, China too. I think of Egon, reckoning his virtual worth, as real estate in the Sahel goes up and down, the

buried and the superficial... And think of all those poor
kids who'll need a drink in Egon's bars.

I need some cash, to start me up.

I have to wait my time, my turn.

'I know you, a soldier won't 'fess up,' I say. 'But,
Marcel, real life involves some truth, some justice – that's
what people think, at least...' He grabs me, shouts,

'You commie bastard. I have dealt with Madame
Feng. Straight as a pin, she is. Her guys are warriors, they
too have nothing to confess. When they pray, it's to what
comes, not to the past...'

'You take a moral twist, Marcel,' I say. 'It isn't what
I want at all. I'm looking for a space where I can be
myself, make you guys listen to my tune...' He turns
away. Then, he has his revelation. 'You – you could
match with Mrs Feng,' he says, 'if she is such a catch.'

'Yes,' I say, 'a catch there is. I saw her in the flesh.
The flesh does not attract – it needs some sorting through,
some re-positioning.'

'The flesh ought not attract,' he says. 'Instead, it is
the symbol, concept – that's what marches on. If you like,
the flag. She – is your human capital. She can buy you –
hoplites. And in return?'

'I've no idea. I've little that I want to give. To pay,' I
say.

The idea – is crass.

He says, 'Hmmm. Russia. China. Unhappy places,
sometimes at least. Though – no place is happy or
unhappy always – unless you believe in hell and heaven.
Even so – language heals: the worst is always followed by
the better. Even a tiny bit: and you've seen the world,
almost all of it: those rusty tin roofs you flew over, the
shacks, like tiny fields of earth, waiting for a seed. Then,

you'll have seen the thatched huts of the Real Life State. All round, the sand, like it's run out from scores of hourglasses. Madame Feng, who's full of history – not only does she change her mind, her mode, like history – she has lived it, and escaped it all. Survivors fool you. They've not experienced the worst, though they have seen it. How they'd like to cleanse and tidy! This empire, America – here you are, you've been drunk in it, urinated, I dare say, where the mood took you. Nothing to be proud in that – it does you credit, though. You flew, an eagle, owl, or albatross. And – you didn't pounce or swoop. Just took it in, cold eye.'

'Yes,' I say, 'it's sad, painful.'

'That's not too bad,' he says. 'You're better working for me, than for Egon. It's all about the Africas we love.'

'It's not work I want,' I say. 'It's cash,' and so we leave it there.

*

Tania says to me, 'With what you do – the bar, the car with us, the burial – you should be gay.'

I say, 'Gay, black, white, women and men – it's just a phase. We'll settle down, decide if we're to share or fight for what is left. Besides – you ate your forecasts, your maquettes. Now that you're devoted to a hopeless love – you could make it as a chef...'

'Oh,' she says, 'that was the symbol, not the stomach.'

'Marcel,' I say, 'longs for decapitation. His eternal life. A guy, on the plane back to here, says all the generals plan for that.'

'He stands a good chance of martyrdom, in Real Life State,' she says. 'Although – he handles the *sadomas* religions well – new science too. He wanted to destroy his body – then see what was left behind. His head! A choice that's really strange!'

'He designed the Real Life,' I say. 'It's normal trade – dressed as utopia. He's something else – neither ordinary, nor a visionary. He's capable of burning tents and shooting camels, without the urging. Not trade, and not utopia.'

'When you look into the future,' Tania says, 'like I did, you see them, two armies – not each fighting one another, but all combat held within... That's why I long for Lia, the peace I ought to want and know she doesn't bring... But – the better it is with her, the less I need her.'

'Lia could have taken us down to Real Life,' I say. 'It needed a driver. We could have gone to see dear Clara – we thought she was so odd, but all she does is look for people who are missing. Now we can't find her.'

'That Madame Feng,' says Tania, starting to whisper. 'Sometimes she's with them – French, Belgians – giving out her packages. But – those guys – their actions seem quite arbitrary. They massacre, they stand aside, they're complicit – they swing round like the moon, they wax and wane. There's never an apology, for what that's worth. I guess there's an account somewhere, profit and loss – and sometimes Mrs Feng herself is on the other side. It seems quite arbitrary too. Where will they all end up, I ask myself. In Marcel's oasis, waiting for Egon to truck in the booze?'

'It's probable for all of them it's arbitrary – and it's calculated,' I say.

'Well,' says Tania, 'it's like me. You know you can't trust me. You can trust Lia, though – she doesn't care about herself so much. I have my reasons, but you don't write books about them.'

'Africa's the test,' I say. 'It's how the future is. You have to be there – not forecasting in my bar.'

'No, no,' says Tania. 'That continent's already fleeing, rolling out. We wouldn't help the guys but our conscience is so large, we'll help some others help them, those Africans who run and swim to flee, who must get out. And Mrs Feng – she makes her buck that way. Her hotel... forever full.'

'Maybe I'm banal,' I say, 'about the future, and which way it lies. Look at Moscow – new buildings everywhere, just like they might have been but for the past, aging cathedrals summoned from way back, time and invention run away, backwards, to start again somewhere, and this time do it better, do it worse. New palaces, faked up to represent a past there never was.'

'People I know said that the DDR must be a punishment,' Tania says: 'rehab. And then – it's over, like it never was. Before it was created – ruins. You'd not begin again from those. And somewhere else, the crime and punishment starts up again...'

'I think we should leave out Africa,' I say. 'We don't know how to take it, where to set our stance. It's not like Lia, needing a dryout, travelling there.'

'No, no,' says Lia, coming in, puffed up, and pulling at our sleeves. 'It's true we're ignorant – but Tania's right. No one would give me autos – they say I break them up too easy. I made do, I was a commentator on TV. So it is with continents – we had our smash, but on we go, spectating, making sense...'

'So, Lia had a job,' says Francine. 'You and Tania are the ones without, and placid too. It would have made sense, if you'd given up on Africa.'

It was all decided. We would stay in France.

Then – our minds are changed. By gravity, by fantasy, by wilfulness...

*

So, here we are, down in the Real Life State, Africa. There is no statue to Adorno. They feel he'd not have wanted one. 'The RLS,' says Marcel, 'is Treasure Island. We are wary of authenticity, and all that stuff. The song says, "Freedom's the recognition of necessity". Well, here, there is no difference. Freedom and necessity are one.'

It's true. Poor Francine – all she says comes out the contrary. She says to stay – at once, we leave. That's the problem – she sells to create emptiness – but something keeps on filling up, her stockhouse, a struggle worse than Sisyphus's, who knew what he was punished for, and at least was certain that eternity would last, and not become extinct like other creeping things.

Here, in Real Life, everybody trades. That is real life, a *do ut des*, real reciprocity. Need, trust, supply. A face to face. Even the priests, the saints, the martyrs too – all into it. The trade's in everything – that strides or hobbles, that you wear or sniff, or shoot or set up in a cage.

'This freedom surpasses everything,' says Tania. A guy says,

'You're from America. You should go back there, since we can't leave here...'

'No, no,' says Tania, 'we are not from anywhere. We're cleansed. Lia was *sans papiers* but she won a race – became a heroine. I was in futurology, and I took fright – but I was into enterprise, it counts, it makes a person of you. You see – we've all experienced the dream, then we awoke, and left. Before we were there, in America, we lived in other civilisations. They have clung. America – should have been the best, but no...' and she points to me, quite boasting. 'We're good – best – at gangs. That's where it leads, the culture.' She turns to me. 'This guy was in the liquor trade, and now he's here to save the birds, and bring the tourists in.'

That's so. There's many who will pay to see the red birds, bet on them, that they will sing. I have my two, all buttoned up, and warm. I think the breed's extinct – that's the attraction. See the last one, like it was that pigeon, or a buffalo.

Here, our species started. If we are lucky, we'll be here, alive, when it all ends. Real Life – the trucks, the packages – they circulate. The animals, the manuscripts, your eyes grow tired with tracking all the deals... and here's a kind of tower, memorial. 'Is it for Clara, or for Clara's son?' asks Lia. 'One or both's a saint, for sure.'

'You see,' Marcel says. 'We don't make commodities here – so there's no alienation, no one gets exploited toiling at the bench or in the mine. It's purest humanism – sell and buy. Two personalities, two characters, as nude as eels, eye to eye, and breath to breath. Egon too – he doesn't have a customer, he doesn't make you drunk, nor happy, nor just in between. His bars are closed – and yet they rise in price, because some guys have figured out the future's rich in booze, the need for it. You see those aloes, over there? – a century, we'll make tequila here, with worms... The question is – you guys, what'll you do? You don't have much to sell...'

'There are no landscapes here,' says Tania. 'Those aloes – they might break the rule that you can't see beyond the bounds. But I can't see the frontier, everything is yellow grit...'

'That's movement,' Marcel says. 'The helicopters and the camels' hooves – they raise the sand, it stops you seeing far ahead.'

'Well,' Tania says, 'I'll not sell my body, if that is what you want. Of course I believe in spirit – those populate the future; that, I saw... But I'm not ready to be spirit yet, and all the guys here – they still have their bodies. If I sell mine, I'd be all spirit, living hypothetically...'

'No, no,' says Marcel, 'you'd not sell a thing. It's just a metaphor. You sell some moments of your time, and in exchange some guy will tell you tales, give confidences... enrich in myriad ways... It's all a humanism, you see. All's on the human plane... of mutual need,' and on he talks.

'Yes, Marcel,' says Tania, 'I am quite convinced, your argument is great – but I won't do it. The intimacy – I hate it. It's a torment: intimacy is just what Lia doesn't give...'

'Yes! Lia,' Marcel says. 'She has speed to sell. We all need that, a tool, component of our traffic here. Perhaps, Tania, Lia has no intimacy to give. If you had it – it'd pall if it were always so, on hand. The presence, content of the intimacy... it would thin out into bland routine. You're better off just wanting, or not wanting it. As for the guys who might want to share your body – that's just illusion. It can't be done. Our body is an island.

No, they want something else, quite innocuous. Probably not for sale either.'

'You don't convince me,' Tania says. 'Does everyone in Real Life argue like this?'

'Oh yes,' Marcel says, 'the guys who're most successful in trade – they've time for theology.'

In theology, there's lots of birds – doves, ravens come to mind. But – they were around. You didn't need to save them.

Marcel goes on, 'Besides, when I was Tania's lover, I never bought a thing – and certainly no part of her. Maybe I ought to have. And now – I don't own a bit of her. Nothing bought, and nothing sold. Of course, then there's Bluebeard and there's Dracula – collectors, hoarders. Not buying, but possession. I'm not into that. I do percentages.'

'What if they don't pay?' I ask.

'They won't do trade here any more,' he says. 'No one cheats. What you think this is – a discount store? No, I watch the commerce, and I do the biggest deals. It's all a balance – there's the Tuaregs, the French, the Yanks, and oil and drugs and stuff that everybody wants, rhinos for Chinese pharmacists... All right and wrong, or partly right or wrong – it doesn't enter into trade.'

'People speed in and out,' says Lia. 'It's how things ought to be. On the move, no one without some goods, being left around to linger round and suffer...'

'Yes,' Marcel says. 'Compassion! None of that! – there never is enough, or, if you like, it's always skewed to this or that wrong side. Everyone should play their part, their interest, and no one chooses sides – it unbalances the ship, our little skiff. You,' and he turns on me, 'Stick to your animals. Forget this searching for the right – you're wrong, you're compromised. You're stereotype. I won't mention Madame Feng, the goods you trucked for her – but there she was, you were.'

'Stone,' says Francine. 'Stones in every hut. So cool.'

'There's no stones around here,' I say.

'There's no kapok either,' Francine says. 'Think of the pyramids. Empty tombs – that's what attracts. Like Clara's. Open it up – maybe it's full of life. Not hers, of course, but breeding in the dark. Stones – when all this place is burned and flat – you'll see them – stone armchairs in the sand.'

'You guys,' I say. 'You make your name with trivia – but it's far beyond me, my powers. I can't compete.'

'You have to know complexity before you make your money with a simple thing,' Francine says, quite kindly. 'Those old guys – they were so delicate. When they went to hell, they made it military – everyone some grade, some punishment defined. Instead, the place is quite arbitrary. There is one hell, and down you go if you were living in a certain place. It doesn't matter what you did, or what you'll do. There is no court, no judgement. All tombs are empty – nothing to gawp at. Below the emptiness – simplicity! That is your deal.'

Lia ferried us all down to Africa – loaded on her dune bike, called a 'Tuareg': now, she says, 'Those stones won't travel – think of all that weight...'

'No, no,' says Francine, quite impatient now. 'You mustn't think of pyramids – those stones – all wasted. All *our* stones have names, a face. Madame Feng brings them in, on diplomatic documents. Some come from Italy, it seems. Stones don't talk – though they do move around.'

'You're a discovery, Francine,' I say. 'These stones too – none of that stuff about liberating the spirit that's within them. They're smooth and cool, you leave them so.'

'Oh well,' she says, 'there's things around we don't want to see come here. The camps. The buses, the people looking out, hoping they'll stop, hoping they won't.'

'We've grown,' I say. 'Once we wanted splendid things – the human suit, the golden helm. Tania – to dance. It's gritty now. We're like some animals who don't eat each other, but gobble all the rest.'

'No,' Francine says, 'here's good. Exchange. No one loitering, with nothing. This way, we'll all be rich.'

'All I want,' I say, 'is someone who sings to me. Every morning.'

'Piano too?' Francine asks. 'Accompanying? All those keys.'

'That. Or an oud. The frets... I haven't thought,' I say. 'A piano takes some space, it needs accommodating. You need some frames to park it in. I don't like architecture much. It must be new, each song, and have an end, that's always reached.'

'It sounds quite easy,' Francine says. 'Me – I can't sing a note.'

'Like me,' I say. 'But that's exactly what it's not about.'

Lia asks, 'Is there a trade in people here?'

'If there is, remember – we're a place of transit. Slavery would be for quite short times. Besides,' says Marcel, 'there's an advantage – slaves don't get fired. Remember all the crap jobs we had, and then we were without, and desperate?'

'The fighting's mostly done by slaves,' says Tania. She turns to me, 'That shootout you were in, you say, that traumatised, and now explains your idleness...'

'*Accidie*,' I correct her.

'...yes, that,' she says. 'I'm sure Marcel can tell us what's the root of all the battling.'

'Oh well,' Marcel expounds, 'the right to bear arms and use them, according to some local rules, and for transcendent goals – that puts the slave and me on equal grounds.' Lia is unconvinced, but Tania says, 'I thought you were reactionary, dear Marcel, but now, you're just an ordinary guy.'

'Too bad,' says Francine. 'The motel huts are never all in use. Stones... they say that "stones do furnish empty rooms".'

'The traders rather sleep outside,' says Marcel, 'with their beasts, or in the trucks. Then, there's the expense...'

I hear Marcel and Tania – in a hut, and having sex quite vigorous. Tania's changing course. That's what the huts are for, just like a real motel.

Lia and I, we watch the Yemenis, the Bokharans – some in flight, and some in business. Then – a relief!

'Hurrah for Madame Feng,' we shout, not thinking twice. Here she is – she stares at us, quite acid. Her brooch, it's bone, it reads 'Khingali'. Here's Alphonse, limping – 'He trod on something with sharp teeth,' Madame Feng explains. 'It's his Achilles syndrome, only temporary.'

'I've just the thing,' I say. Mrs Feng – she sings, morning, evening too, but she is not for me. 'Francine can make a chair, Alphonse'll ride in it – you just need robust guys...' But she's impatient.

'There is new wealth here – Marcel's installed, and Egon's not nomadic,' says Mrs Feng, angry now. 'He's burrowing for his properties. And here – there's too many want percentages. My humanitarian work is compromised...'

Marcel and Tania exit from their hut, Tania like Mélisande, twirling her purple wraps.

'You two – you're ganging up,' says Madame Feng, thrusting Lia, now aghast, towards them. 'But I shall not forget that barman, even though he's trickled through his hourglass. There is a rule of law. Marcel will not slough it off...'

'Of course we have the law,' Marcel says. 'But we have justice too. Justice as fairness. Nothing legalistic. Forgetting is a cardinal point – a human trait. It's only fair that we forget what's past. After all, it isn't there...'

Madame Feng's impressed. 'Yes,' she says. 'That's the kind of argument I need. But everywhere there's empty rooms, and empty huts. Egon – has empty bars. We have to fill them up, or else – percentages of nought is nought,' and Alphonse nods.

'Tania – what's all this crap?' shouts Lia. 'The future, love... And now, there and back again – screwing the big boss in the dust – Oh Tania! Our fable ends, though I was never truly part...' She throws a punch at Tania, Marcel fends it off... In his hand he has a football helmet, maybe to placate good Madame Feng – 'Oh yes,' says Madame Feng. 'How diplomatic! From the losers and the lame, I came to pick my team. The latest rules require that you don't run. Scurrying around – that sends the message "panic", "flee" – not what we want.'

I remember the static redheads, losing their game. 'People watch anything,' says Madame Feng. 'Guys starving in boxes, just for fun. Stars who're fallen, just down visiting. Football's the only thing that's not a metaphor – everything on earth is metaphor, but for that,' and Alphonse nods again.

Francine has measured him. She picks his rock, and here's a couple of the guys who'll carry him – 'Shoulder high!' shouts Madame Feng. '*Davai, davai*! Onward, upward, vengeance shall be his!'

'We're all fascinated by this place,' she says. 'There's arms and drugs – but no one shoots or sniffs. There ought to be a polity – but everyone is on the move, no one is ruled or subject – punishments you settle with some cash; the left, the right – are stirred together in a ratatouille. We powerful cheeses take percentages – for noble aims, of course – according to the flow of trade...' she pauses, cautiously.

'The answer is, dear Madame Feng – they don't need guys like you at all,' says Lia, throwing stuff at Tania.

'Of course they do,' says Madame Feng. 'There's all humanity to cure. It calls. Alphonse's foot.'

'No problem, Madame Feng,' says Alphonse, hoisted up. 'Beware anarchic rant. There's order in all this – it's just it works so well, it doesn't strike you all at once.'

'If you guys want courts and law,' says Marcel, irritated. 'We'll set it up. Tania – you're knowledgeable about love, and passion too. You'll evaluate emotions, and all that. Francine – you deal with quantities and weights. You'll set the penalties. You two can be the judges.'

'We'll be judging you, Marcel,' says Tania. 'You'll hop and squawk!'

Lia says, 'Tania – passion is quite what you lack. You'd never catch me! Not with your sticky web...' and weeps.

'Do what you will,' says Marcel. 'In my case there's neither love nor quantity involved.'

I'm tired of this. Tania's dialogs, Marcel's measured steps, Madame Feng and her good works.

I find Egon. 'There's much superficiality around,' I say. 'I don't know how I can avoid it, but it's not the direction that I want.'

'That's right,' Egon says. 'You need to remember what the song says, "*Je suis comme je suis*". Even when you wilt under your years. Don't bother with anyone but yourself.'

'I agree,' I say, 'though that's not quite what I had in mind.'

'I have customers now,' says Egon. 'I have to jolly things along. More majesty, and more profound. That shallow line. Even shallow sounding deep turns most guys off.'

'You almost have a landscape here,' I say. 'There's ups and downs. You might take a photograph, to show the guys when they are far inside your bar.'

'The trouble is,' says Egon, sweating, stooped. 'I dig and dig real deep – and I can't find my properties. There's every kind of good down there, but not my bars. It's not that I'd sell alcohol...'

I don't offer to dig, though he makes to give me a spade.

'The riches here,' he says, 'makes me almost think there's a divinity – who doesn't care for us. His mind is on the chain, on how it hangs. Maybe He has a fantasy, about a monstrous woman, breasts like the milky way –

on whose neck he hangs the chain. Maybe He's hermaphrodite. Or when it's dark, takes out Her jewels to scatter in the sky... Vanity, oh vanity! Is it all for that? Myself – I haven't broken any necklace – but – I ask myself, is it the length, the extent, cohesion, that makes the chain a chain? Or is it the pearls, the spacers? Is it all stuck together, or composed of tiny bits that takes a mind to compose it all and grasp...' He would go on. I say – 'The chain's a chain, whichever way.' My answer disappoints.

'If the divinity cannot repair what we have broke,' says Egon, spading into sand, 'the baubles and the string will fly as cinders to oblivion. Leaving Her – resentful, furious, vindictive to us all. That anger, the scorn, will send us massed together, into the boiling stewpot...'

'Hugo thought about the chain. Not about God, providence, destiny, motive... Rather, a General Secretary...' I say.

'Nonsense,' Egon says. 'We broke it. We broke it once for all, a glue job means we'd know the trick, how to fudge repairs. And do it all again.'

'So, if you find a bar, Egon,' I say, 'wear your helm, and serve strong booze.'

'I could do the story as an opera,' says Egon, 'if I find an amphitheatre, down underground. But suppose it's been done before?'

'Marcel did Great Books,' I say. 'He'd know. Though devastation myths are popular all round.'

'No myth,' says Egon. 'I've been in the futures trade – I know.'

'To put it on the stage,' I say, 'there's only one way, one formula: "We must be proud – to break the chain, mend it, or pray to it – it's all the same. We're in command, we're free, we're independent. No God, no tsar, and no heroes..."'

'You can't end a song that way,' says Egon. 'That's your empty room, even if it's full of people. The story must go on, not end in endings that are hypothetical.'

'Dig, Egon!' I say. 'Find the chain of bars.'

'Well,' he says, 'we're still the lucky ones. We're opening up the world – and this here, is its toughest part.'

'I'm not even sure of that,' I say. 'Though – Marcel's taken up with Tania. She's his judge, with Francine. Lia's been deserted twice. And you've no future, Egon. As for me – maybe I'll go on trial myself.'

'A straight path's an illusion,' Egon says. 'You see it – till you see no more, no further. Your eye, just like the earth, is round. A straight line's only relative. Curvature – it brings us back, as though we never left. We'll come through, back into the future. All of us, us friends...'

'Lia's religion – that has no straights,' I say. 'She chose one like the track – chicanes, twists, curves. Or maybe just endurance, no race, no movement of any kind, just pictures, like a simulator, turning the wheel. Keeping the image, the target in your eye...'

'That's poetry,' says Egon, 'but digging doesn't fit with it. Give me a hand, if you can't give me peace.'

I persist, 'Lia chose the wrong religion, for her temperament.'

'Two women judges,' Egon says. 'That's a strong statement right away. I'd be a militant myself, a prophet even – but my record isn't all that clean. and then – my assets – some lie in revolutionary lands. They're out of reach for prudent guys, like me...'

'Not all those revolutions are what I had in mind,' I say. 'Still less what Hugo planned. There's initiatives arrive from every angle – the grassroots, tall poppies, popes, and preachers in the bush. You need flies' eyes to watch your back.'

'Forget all that,' says Egon. 'You – we – aren't part of it. Marcel keeps peoples who don't like each other much, dependent, swapping stuff; rubbing along, wood on wood, steel on steel. It doesn't lead to riches. No one makes anything – they just truck along. Trade mixes up the cultures, that's what they say. It makes a kind of dough. But, I told you, the gods love networks, especially the threadbare ones. Networks. That's what I have, if I could only find it... them.'

'You both have states behind you,' I say, grasping everything: the big system, the mechanism, Madame Feng and all.

'It's activity attracts them,' Egon says. 'States. A stirring, and they're on you. You knew all that. States destroy, and states protect. Marcel won't come to trial – besides, he's only seen off a squad of undistinguished guys. Not lovely, either.'

'Hugo wanted revolution. But he wanted his good state as well,' I say.

Egon says, 'Lia's the one for you – her game was real. She's not piloted a drone. When some guys go out of sight, in all this sand – who knows what falls on them? Lia did the racing all for fun, and for herself.'

'They watch us all the time,' I say. 'That's why there are no landscapes. No perspective. That's all bled out on the screen.'

'You must be realist,' says Egon, starting on another hole, spading the sand into the previous one. 'Not distrust what everybody sees but you. Now they've built a courthouse – it's something they can burn, along with flags – those mournful spots and stripes. When that time comes, jump on the back of Lia's bike, and – as Marcel says – just "flee the scene".'

'There's little in this scene to flee,' I say.

'It's worn out, that's all,' says Egon, cheerfully. 'There's lots must have happened here, you can make fantasies about all that – the gardens, the nobles, and the faithful *demos*, waiting for the curtain's up.'

I say, 'Egon – you and Marcel were together in the army. You both must understand the past, the future too.'

'Yes, of course,' he says. 'We repented, naturally, after, but there's no procedure for regret. So were you. In it too.'

'It was another army, I remember well,' I say, although I don't, I'm not that sure. I may have said I was. We marched. We had no guns. 'Arise', we said.

'The military – it gave Marcel body, substance. It's about negotiation – maybe everything is that.' I say. 'We all had once to be in armies. Some we belonged to from our birth.'

'That's how you learn to dig,' says Egon, getting on with it. 'Part of learning to be on your side.'

'A guy comes through,' I say. 'Selling monkeys that can sniff out gold. Maybe they could adapt and find your nickel bar-rails.'

'Try anything,' says Egon.

I see Lia, on her dune bike, carrying Marcel's cashbags to the bank.

I ask Marcel, 'Isn't it too risky?'

'Banks always are,' he says. 'And – it's Lia's passion, riding to countries all around. And she loves risk.'

'Quick! Get on!' shouts Lia. 'I bounce too much. I need a dead weight.'

'You need a stone, from Francine,' I say, offended, climbing on.

'No,' says Lia, 'I need a talking stone, one that invents a name. For the account.'

'Phineas Micawber,' I say immediately.

There's a sign – 'Republic of...' and we're past. 'The name is good, forgotten already,' she says. 'Now we need a bank.'

Here there's nothing.

'Oh yes,' she says, 'there's always something. You need the eye. Here there's a theatre. Those would be the tops of mango trees, here's empty wells, and mineshafts full of 'forty-niners. It's all gone under, but it's there.'

'And Egon's bars?' I ask. There's silence. Groups of guys with guns – they wave us on. We're both of colour indeterminate. Agnostics in most religions. We don't arouse the warriors.

Up and down, sleek as silverfish in parchment folds, we ride. There is no landscape. Either there's no horizon – or it's all horizon. 'Shout when you see a bank!' shouts Lia. 'If we get stuck, there's nothing here can save us. You see – you wanted nothing, *tabula rasa,* so's you could start again. A clean sheet. But here – "nothing" will do for you, it's fatal. Men will rob you as you croak. If they're kind, they'll cut your parched throat as they leave.'

'There's a bank over there,' I shout. 'It says "Fargo", and there's a figure with little pinions on its heels.'

'That must be the manager, making off!' says Lia. 'It's a mirage. Your tame imagining!'

We race past the bank. Not seeing things that's there – those must be Lia's mirages. 'Oh, for the open road,' she sings. 'My sad sack on the pillion...'

'You could give the cash to Madame Feng,' I say. 'Good works. The envelopes.'

'Marcel thinks she is a criminal,' Lia says. 'Over the line, that is, that makes you criminal, even when there is no law. Poor guys – they take the cash and settle loans that make guys rich. That's what she says, at least. Then they owe her. Or, she makes a deal that makes guys give up arms, makes it easy for the ones who don't... here, you need a gun, or a fast bike...'

'It's a stereotype again,' I say. 'There's lots of guys here, working stiffs, no pistol and no bike. One day, they'll all be rich.'

'Of course they will,' she says. 'Mine was just a joke.'

I move my hands up to cover her breasts. We drive on, faster, faster, in silence.

Then there's a tree – its fronds metallic, the rest genuine. A store, '*Les choses de la vie*' it says. A row of banks. 'We put a little in each till,' says Lia.

'No,' I say. 'We must be bold, bet everything on one.'

Here's the best – you open an account, they give you a cute red plastic bird. 'This is the one,' I say.

'You're obsessed by ones,' says Lia. 'One bank, one person that is right for all your moods. Find yourself a cure!'

'One's an advance on nought,' I say. I put the bird in with the other two.

Nothing happens here, except for thought. Then, there's the raid, and those that live are on the move.

'The Real Life State should have its bank,' I say.

'You don't appreciate it, maybe,' Lia says. 'But there is class war in Real Life, as well as all the other things. A bank is tempting to incendiaries, even if inside it holds just scrawls and scribbles.'

Without the cash, we're lighter now. We fly from bump to lump.

We're vertical. We fall. Our heads clash, mine like the clapper of the bell against her helmet.

'There!' she says. 'We almost flew. Instead, we've trashed the bike.'

I'm dazed. Her head has spilled itself in mine. Speed, faster and faster – I say, 'The universe is ponderous. It should be speeded up – not just extinctions of the crawling things, but of stars and moons and atmospheres. Not years, but seconds. Not millennia – but hours. Get it done, and quick – this lingering, it makes you weep.'

'Of course,' she says. 'When you go fast, you either hit the wall, or else the space. Crash or freedom, that's the thing.'

'So, Lia, what becomes of this? The Beau Geste. The free state? Contradictions... syntheses, all that,' I ask.

'Oh well,' she says, 'When they have dug out all this sand and made cement of it, they'll find the theatres and the rocks, and put in trees and stores, and red birds – virtual... And put our bones into a case and light them up, and write them into stories on those tiny cards that no one reads...'

'It's all destroyed?' I ask. 'We're driven off – if that's our luck; and Clara's mausoleum – mud and straw, will disappear...'

'That is the way,' she says. 'Get used to it. Now, we will have to push the bike. And – where's my commission? You too deserve a token sum...'

'I didn't think,' I say. 'It all went in the bank, that manager, Mister Redwing was his name – he said religion stopped him giving a receipt. The bank's name... Flyaway Finance, or some such thing...'

'You cretin,' Lia shouts. 'All forgotten! I can't trust you... What will Marcel say?'

And on she shouts, our tender moment seeps away.

She's scuffing at the bike, like a dog hiding some ugliness. It starts – she's off. I scream after her, 'I – I've remembered...' but she doesn't hear. The helmet stoppers up her ears... My shout – clears me of misogyny and theft: – I spoke, she didn't hear. That's why our species never gets to heaven. The cash can all be mine – the question is – who'd I have stolen from? The traders? Marcel? Lia? all those – or probably: Nobody. That's how Odysseus got away, and met his fate – eternity... with Penelope, the weaver of deceit, the faithless textile worker.

As they say, 'theory doesn't boil an egg'. But while you're wrestling with that – it lets you on to something else – and as you register your torrid sweats in this new heat, how can you boil your egg, if one you find? Real Life – it's what they call corrupt, but that won't make the world rotate. No, that's another theory. But – the money's mine, potentially. I need it, and I want it. Maybe it's a right. I see the hut, far off, where Marcel is on trial. My journey back to Real Life – it's all a mirage. Banks come into it, and cliffs of alabaster, the eggnog from the Empty Room... In the shelter of Lia's breasts I lay me down... mirage is a wonderful release. Then, camel bells, and sheep. I crawl. I'm home.

Tania and Francine take off their crow clothes, their judges' togas: blindfold and naked, they raise their wings, and free Marcel. 'No body, no crime,' they sing. They croak.

'A celebration, then,' says Marcel, about to bear his justices to bed, prepare a vindictive screw. 'Better than innocence is – absolution. I'm not just guiltless, nothing I do is visible... Mine, the unseen hand, the finger that excites...'

'I feared you'd died,' Lia says to me. 'And I searched for you,' she lies. 'Clara. Her spirit has guided you...'

'Tyre tracks,' I don't say.

I pat the plastic redbird. I pour water in myself. We're all mud. Lenin – or Hugo – would have said – 'Chistka! Must get the mud out the Party!'

'A discrete party,' Marcel says. 'By way of sacrifice. My trial is done.'

Lia pulls Tania and Francine from the hut. They're dressed again as justices. Lia says to me, 'Your mind is colonial,' and to Marcel, she says, 'You're no Napoleon. We shan't have a modern state, all glued to the one song. No, it'll be traditional. No oil. So, no modernity. Everything depending on our characters – every one. Even Egon. But not him,' and she points at me. 'He's excluded. Not to be trusted. Too much silence.' The others stare.

Marcel doesn't know about his cash.

'How do you judge good Madame Feng?' I ask.

'Oh,' says Lia, thinking fast. 'She's the pearl in the oyster, the tar in the honey. She has a body too. And – a traditional state – we base it on the body.'

'Mine's finely tuned,' says Marcel, laughing and throwing his up and down.

'The body, yes,' says Lia. 'But clean, pure, and abstemious. sleeping on the floor, fasting for days. That way, you win respect – down here on earth as well.'

It's good to feel austere.

'This here,' says Marcel, 'is not a city, that strange, haunted place – here, no deep-thinking humorous guys are passing through. Don't ask the traders what they're carrying. If they say "crocodile" – it's animals, not dope. To talk with them, I've a new language, new sanctions too. I speak in many tongues, and ask no credit for it. Simplicity, not double meanings,' and on he talks.

The acrobats are coming through – those from Tunisia, with muscles; Tanzanians – they're contortionists – it's not exactly trade they're in. Rather, travelling and twisting...

'No, no, Francine,' shouts Tania. 'Don't chisel on your stones. That way they become commodity – that way, we run into trouble. Sedentaries arrive. Then cities. The flag – that is enough. Leave out the rest.'

'Tania,' says Francine, hurt, 'I am an artist. That's my job – to sell and chisel.'

'Be satisfied with jurisprudence,' Tania says. 'You've exonerated Marcel, higher than that you cannot go. No one looks at patterns when they're sat on them. Look at me – I saw the future – now, I won't go further than today. It's called the *Zeitgeist*, taking it slow and easy, one hour at a time.'

'What's all this nonsense?' Madame Feng exclaims. 'This place was always gossamer. Its beauty is – ephemeral. You should enjoy that, not invent, not justify.'

I love them all, each in their way. They're my friends. There's no one else, not here. But maybe Madame Feng is closest to me. Not a friend, just close; not honest, she's straight as nails. Burned out, like all around here, used up, but still an inspiration.

And if it rains – desert flowers, desert storms. Here – extra prayers, covering up, it's something new. Watching punishments, death, mutilation. In the city, everyone has other things to do. But here – there's nothing else. It would all be fresh. Something to see, until it palls. Down with Clara's mausoleum, down with her freaky son! There's time, centuries, to build it up again. And the trade – that must go on.

'Those Tunisians – they stood on each other's shoulders – stole the flag,' says Egon, trembling. It's a portent.

'It's not they're Tunisians on the lam,' Marcel says, 'I have no prejudice, no preference. It's that they're acrobats. Nothing to sell, except themselves. Not true proletarians – just showbiz. The worst of all the worlds this delicate spot seeks to avoid.'

Everything's a portent. You never know what you won't recover from.

'Hey,' Francine says to me, 'this is serious. We're vulnerable. You ought to snap out of your numb feeling, your *accidie* – shootouts are over quick, you can't brood on them. Forget!'

'It's not a shootout that afflicts me,' I say, 'it's the experience: you're alive but didn't quite survive.'

'It really sounds quite trivial,' Francine says.

'It is, it is,' I say. 'It's like us, one by one, that's what we are: quite trivial.'

'Oh well,' she says, 'sit on your mystery.' She turns to them all. 'This guy – thinks his small hurt is manageable. Exile? Being thrown out of one place means you get to enter in another one – a better one. You never lose. Your origins, your life – it's all a shimmering sack of silk, it trails behind you, smelling of closed rooms. He doesn't know how usual he is, the loss – it's so tiny, it's invisible.' She reaches the point: 'But – losing a flag is drastic. It puts us all at risk.'

Most guys here – they went through wars and camps, and being chased. They trek on – like me, they've not survived.

Tania tells me, 'We didn't absolve Marcel. He's guilty. We couldn't decide on specifics – Francine couldn't anyway. He's guilty, that's all.'

'People disappear around everyone,' I say, 'but you, Tania – you've moved outside people, all of them. You live in the *Zeitgeist* – time's ghost.'

'Marcel did things, things that make you guilty, though yourself – you don't feel it,' Tania says ignoring me. 'Guilty – that's good, definitive. You can do what you like with that, once it's established. I'm with the Tuaregs now. I love them, see them pass by, and I'm glad I'm not one of them, don't need to have a clan.'

'Judgments don't mean much to me,' Marcel says: 'If I need, I can call on a real army. It has no nationality – though it's French. Order, peace – and Madame Feng. I must persuade poor Egon – to do a deal with her. Build a resort. Stop digging for lost wealth. Into the new. Time to place ourselves on the people's side.'

We look out over the two-tone panorama. Probably we see – first, the rough unusual place. Then, the people coming in, demanding water.

'That flag,' says Madame Feng, 'it could be planted somewhere else, set up some more Real Life. If you wanted,' she says to me, 'you could transfer there. Be an *archon*. You could follow in the tracks of those Tunisian acrobats...'

'I don't have the human touch,' I say. 'Not like Clara. And I'd need a truck. A bike. For the removal.'

'Nonsense,' says Madam Feng. 'Alphonse could bear you on his back, you'd be his curse. Clara – she was a martyr: that, you should avoid! All too human, Clara was – and so martyred herself, like all who redeem the soaks and toxics. Alas, me too. My good works...'

Is that a tear she tries to shed?

It's not my idea. Another settlement? I recoil from it – but it shakes me up. I rouse myself, denounce a couple... The guy, a magician, with a bear dragged on a string, the woman – his assistant... Their act, it seemed, not clean.

Alphonse says, 'Yes, that's the way. Be rigorous, even if you're wrong. What happens next to them – is certainly not up to you.'

'It was the bear who danced,' I say to Tania. 'Against nature. Lumbering around...'

'Oh, don't apologise on my account,' she says. 'Dancing on your own – it's out of date.'

Francine says, 'Madame Feng has her eye on that animal, the bear. She wants him as a mascot – one of her teams. The Americans – they long to fight the Russians – then they'll take on the Chinese. It's all about new rules. Bears go down big in China – medical research, all that. The football – that will inflate as well. It takes new formulas, that's all. New rules.'

'Marcel might want to stage a tournament,' says Tania. 'Egon can do the catering.'

'Oh, absolutely not,' says Francine. 'That's your forte, Tania. You should theme this place. Each team's hut shaped just like its country – and then, it eats its neighbours' food. The mascots – make a park for them. Brazilian agate – that can be the trophy...'

'You need to write this down,' says Tania, irritated. 'Your mind is far too rich – it's just a game, and you've broke through into history and politics, Francine.'

'The bear is dead,' says Lia.

'No,' I say, 'it has to stand because they mutilate its hands.'

'Keep it with you,' Lia says. 'You're the ecological. You collect the wounded. It's about to be extinct. It's *à rebours*. Make it so it doesn't dance. Back into nature, clean.'

'Why don't you race again, Lia?' Francine asks. 'Over the dunes, on your Tuareg bike?'

'None of us will go with you, Lia,' Tania says. 'It's all up to you, for you alone. Francine here – she has her business. My business – is with Marcel.'

'I'd need a lot of bikes,' says Lia, showing some doubt. 'And a crew. Two crews, one fixed, one mobile.' We all turn away.

'Egon will succeed,' says Francine. 'The resort! Rough tourism! No sedentaries, of course, just people passing through; not into trade.'

'Yes,' Egon says. 'Shoppers. Archaeologists, ethnographers. Conflict-resolvers of all stripes and spots. I hate them. Hate them all.'

'You put them up, and put up with them, Egon,' I say: 'Some guys, down Hugo's way – they had their enemies on the run. Then it was non-violence and "excuse me". They could have ended all this culture stuff, "respect the differents", feeling good... All that. They could have shaken things up, the world turned downside up. Power to the powerless. They stopped too soon. Then – the copout, "serve the people".'

'Well then,' says Tania, 'what about the Tuaregs? If you had had your way?'

'Not me,' I say, 'Hugo. I just follow things along, hypothetically. I'm a tiny fish, scared of the net. The Tuaregs? whatever's done to them, they'll end up the same. End bad, just end. Whatever they may try.'

'Violence has a terrible poor aim,' says Marcel. 'It spatters. The bad guys live on – they're our warning, not to hope too much.'

There's no reply to that, nor to Marcel. 'I remember being happy,' I say, moving us along. 'That's not so easy here.'

'You've less substance than the rest of us,' says Tania. 'You have no eye for life, just as it comes.'

'I could give that bear a slab,' says Francine. 'Just for reclining. The *mago* and his friend – where have they gone?'

'Oh,' Marcel says, 'they disappeared. That's best for them, out of the light. Whether or not you believe in magic – they were suspect. That was their trade, to be seen through, mistrusted! Who knows what they could make to disappear? Better they end up where we cannot go and do not know. It saves us empathy. Like Clara's son. He disappeared. How did it all happen? It's beyond science, that.'

They look at me. 'I was in the bar,' I say. 'I know nothing. It's all a mystery.'

Madame Feng whispers to Lia: maybe she'll fund those bikes? Gloves for the bear? Maybe she needs cash taken to the bank.

Lia goes off.

Madame Feng says, 'It's perilous here. But – if nobody wants you here – you don't get closed down. The nobodies, and what they don't want: – they cancel each other out,' and she laughs. We find her impenetrable, but we laugh too, in hope.

'Off she goes!' says Madame Feng, and, to me, 'Your companion, Lia.' We watch the smoke from her bike, until she is obscured by fumes and wind. 'You see,' Madame Feng says to me, 'You're wrong, quite wrong. I seek to empty rooms so's I can fill them up, and move away, and so, and so: onward, all over again. You, old friend, just want an empty room to occupy, to start to seek again. But what you seek is you yourself. Empty yourself – then see what's left to find.'

'Madame Feng,' I say, 'you put it well. But – you're sentimental. Trite. Sequins on tinsel. We start empty. You can't fill up yourself with you! There is no quest. Travelling brings you back to where you were. No, it's the shock, the new, the unexpected alien...'

I have my birds.

I have the flag. Those Tunisian acrobats – they'd have no use for it. I fill my pocket with it. It's precious signs.

'All we can be certain of,' says Egon. 'Is power. "Who whom". The rest – "Who are you?", "Why?", "What" – is inconclusive, music.'

'Lia will be back, I guess,' says Tania. 'She maybe went off to the bank. She worked hard on her character – then she saw, she could do nothing here.'

'She wouldn't steal,' says Francine. 'Not Marcel's cash. Maybe – invest. She was at home with bets and such.'

'I'm sure you're right, Egon,' I say. 'The thing is, especially in this place, we don't know "who whom"; who has what you call power. Maybe that explains why Lia's gone.'

They ignore this – at least, they don't take it up.

We never see Lia again.

*

'I won't tell Marcel about Lia and the bank,' says Tania. 'Not unless it becomes a strategic case.'

We have no defence. Only Marcel's diplomacy. We await his summons, made when they are upon us – an army? A band of warriors? Friends, foes?

'Lia won't come back. They'll have stolen her bike. She'd be out of gas. Lost. Burnt. It's strange to lose a lover in this way,' says Tania. 'There's no place for us here. We've nothing useful. Waiting for the wave to sweep us away,' and she laughs. 'No waves here for centuries.'

'I'm for holy war. At least – for holy resistance,' Egon says. 'Remember, the banks they robbed in Tiflis? The cathedals – dynamited! Think of Yaroslavl' – there was a gesture! Those Bolshie guys – wanted everybody to be educated. Now, these guys see it the other way around. They have a point. Reading and writing. And here we are. Enlightened, desperate. All these guys we see – what will they eat? What fuel will they use? They don't care you're on a diet, Francine. They don't know there's Lion Bars in New York, where you can have a tiger steak...'

'I'm not getting out,' says Madame Feng. 'Though Alphonse says it's time. People don't leave, not even when it's past the time.'

'Lia will turn up, for sure,' Marcel says. 'Even if it isn't here, unknown to us. She's famous. She had a tie to Egon, and to Tania – ties don't break. Those kinds of ties – they're not material, so they can't be broke, no matter exists to break them, no whetstone, no steel, no glass paper. She's still connected,' and he goes on, expounds his thought.

'Yes,' says Francine, 'Those who loved her loved themselves a portion more, and so she's entered in to us, and we go on, and there's the chain, it never breaks...'

'Francine,' says Tania, 'you have a squalid mind. It's a jeweller's shop where nothing's priced above a buck.'

'This tournament,' says Madame Feng. 'We had the blacks against the whites, and now the browns are up against the blacks. Really! No wonder Alphonse thinks the rules are wrong! They all eat each others' food, and steal their songs. Where does that bear come in, I ask?'

'We must have mascots, Madame Feng,' says Francine. 'He came from Turkey.'

'I'm off!' says Alphonse. 'There's here too many rules, and none are set by me. I'll have Lia send a postcard, if I see her – though there's no delivery...'

'No, no!' screams Madame Feng, suddenly inflamed, pulling Alphonse from his truck and kicking at his head. 'Rules! It's the routine, the ordinariness – the portal to the horrors! A newcomer, a different prayer, a burial upside-down – that's all it takes... Then, we're running off – into the sun, the bush – the guys with guns will shoot, the guys with penises will shoot them at what moves... whoever has a match will burn the huts, the corn, whoever's impure will poison all the wells...!'

'But, Madame Feng,' says Francine. 'It was rules you wanted. For the football, the tournament. So's Egon could open eateries. We could all have fun, and cheer.'

'No, no,' shouts Madame Feng. 'Not rules! The right rules! Not custom, not routine. Not following orders. Other rules, the right ones.'

'Calm, Madame Feng,' says Alphonse. 'Just beyond where you can see – there's rivers, of folks that's running up and down...'

'Don't look! Don't look!' shouts Madame Feng. 'I know all that! I told you – routine's enough to bring on massacres!'

'I think you kicked me in my sight,' says Alphonse, gazing at the sun. 'I'll need to drive by instinct. Good there is no road, and no direction, and no goal. I'll drive until I hit.'

'You haven't understood,' says Madmae Feng, relaxing. 'Any system, and theory, brings forth rules. That's what my envelopes were for...'

'I thought they were for paying off some guys and persecuting the backsliders,' Alphonse says.

'Yes, that as well,' says Madame Feng.

'But will you help the guys out there?' asks Francine, waving towards what we can't quite see.

'That's not the point,' says Madame Feng.

'Will you save the world? The continent? At least, our part?' asks Tania.

'How should I know?' asks Madame Feng. 'No, I doubt it. My humanitarian work is not for the impossible, the present, the universal. It's for another chapter, new characters. It is pro tem, it claims no more.'

'My advice, good Madame Feng,' says Alphonse, climbing back into his truck. 'Is come with me. Guide me. My retribution – it can wait, until we're both in safety.'

Tania whispers to me, 'Alas! Madame Feng's the only one who has a strategy, and tells us how we should behave. And we can't understand her.'

'It's clear, she doesn't like the guys who leave before their time,' I say. 'Maybe she'll bring some new guys in...'

And, maybe, Lia waits for me behind the bank.

'People here – they're used to being shunted round,' says Marcel. 'Or else, they've done the shunting. Me – I shall remove myself from you, my friends. I'll wear my mask – it ought to be of gold, but, being just of skin, it will reinforce, double, my humanity...'

'Here's another,' says Madame Feng, when Marcel takes his leave, 'who sidles out, having prepared a safe retreat.' She looks round us, suspiciously. 'That perfid Alphonse won't get far,' she says. 'I was to fill his truck with gas, but I forgot. The first time in my life that I forgot a thing!' She laughs. 'He won't get far, but it should be far enough.'

'We're like the Indians,' Francine says, 'waiting for our camp, for somewhere we'll be parked.'

'That's nonsense, Francine,' Tania says. 'We came, if not as conquerors, as guys who patch things up, who fix.'

I'm used to exile. It's a permanent thing, to come from a poor place, and end up poor, from a place with no land and no road, to another. All in all, it's good, it's home.

'Has Marcel really gone?' Francine asks. 'Sitting alone, wrapped in that skin, the barman's face tied on to

his, no longer a disguise – expecting some superior force
to rip it off? And Madame Feng – playing soccer with
poor Alphonse's head!'

'Alphonse is used to that,' says Madame Feng.
'Besides, he won't come back. He should be sending me
two more...' She fumbles for the word – the first time in
her life a word's escaped.

'Missionaries?' Francine suggests.

'Operatives,' says Madame Feng. 'Marcel is prudent.
If he has to save his skin – he has a spare if needed. And
you, Francine – your colour – that's the most precious
thing about you. Red gold. Don't think you can linger
here, trading your stones. This land is needed, empty, or
full. It's strategic. That's why I'm here. But – we are so
few. The best have left. Lia wore poor Egon's helm – but
if she falls – a helm's no use on sand. And if she walks –
her head will fry in it.'

Poor Lia. Maybe she yet waits...

'Whoever gets a lot of power,' says Madame Feng,
pinning her eye on Egon. 'It brings out the animal in
them. Or – they just become more animal... There's
Marcel – a sideways stroller, the mollusc seeking the
crab's empty shell, and hiding in it. Others – well, the
wolves! The different kinds of dog, that humans have
devised – unaware, a quest to designate the species of the
powerful! Little wormy snappers, lop-eared hunters, randy
mongrels with their pizzles hanging out... the barboncini
with their frizzled hair, white afros, the boxers cut down
to ride the blows: and spates of terriers – elected barkers...
But there's other kinds, more noble, less incontinent – the
elks, the elephants, the antelopes. Weight and skills – but
my! All the greenery they eat!'

'These designer creatures,' Francine says, amazed. 'It isn't love they seek! It's all to have a quasi-politician on a lead, to take for strolls?'

'Of course, my dear,' says Madame Feng, pleased to have her *boutade* taken up.

'I should have gone to the Juilliard,' Francine continues – 'Instead of in the furniture biz. And – will we all survive? This experience...'

'Francine,' I say, 'with a face like yours, you'd never act. And – of course this cannot last. What do you expect, dynasties? Me, I found it all quite positive – the bar, the drink, the *noir* and dodging hoods in France. Then this... It's all Real Life, Francine. You don't get that in drama school, and you don't need to find the fees...'

Francine's unsure. The others nod.

Madam Feng repeats, 'They'll all be rich if they follow my way.' The others keep nodding. It's a plausible thing to say: she goes on, 'Marcel called on the army. If you don't possess a gun, you seek a big solid building to hide in – and that's what armies target. I hope they haven't damaged trade.'

We all hope that.

Francine's a good sort, I wish I liked her more. She sees me staring at her, 'Surely you miss something here?' she says. 'Don't you dream of something else?'

'Like "*le son du cor au fond du bois*"?' I say, 'You seek the place where you need the least in order to survive.'

'Clara's rehab refuge,' Tania says. 'That was fasts and silences. Watching tiny beasts scutter into holes. She did it cheap, to save for her mausoleum.'

'Rehab slowed Lia down,' says Egon. 'Maybe it was a bad idea. Clara's for sure a saint – but why'd she need a massive tomb?'

'It was for her son, and anyone who looked like him,' I say.

'Well, it gets knocked down – we'll build it up again,' says Egon, his head pale gold, with nodules, as though it's repoussé, with who knows who inside, hammering it round. 'You can't have people making new countries, fighting religious wars, and kidnapping guys,' he says. 'I guess. It's been done before. Anyway, we're a squad. We'll work it out.'

'You quite understood a while ago,' I say. 'A war becomes necessity – you want it, maybe, or anyway it comes.'

'You understand,' he says. 'And then you understand the other side. We were taught that.'

We could take people in, protect them. Thinking of Hugo, of Lia – we're not that good at it. Still, we could try with that tall guy, who sets his son to steal, food and other things, the woman, her daughter with bent legs... They make their plea. Marcel's off, doing diplomacy next door. Still, the four of us, plus Madame Feng – we are a team. But people here – they differ so. If we take in one lot, another lot will feel left out.

'You need to know who are the principals,' says Egon. 'Who's behind the army, for example. Those empires... the Romans, they stopped being soldiers, went to fight-clubs, then to church. A lesson there for all of us! So, the mercenaries, the semi-citizens – they did the wacking, but the orders came from up somewhere...'

'Everybody else – they called barbarians,' says Tania. 'It worked for ages.'

'I've a mind,' says Madame Feng. 'To seek another Mister Feng. Alphonse has gone for good, or ill. I'd go among the Sahrawis and search – they're loyal and patient, and they have a lovely flag.'

'I'd no idea,' says Francine, 'that you and Alphonse were a pair... Madame Feng, you must be torn to shreds.'

'Oh no,' says Madame Feng. 'There's no original of Mister Feng. I'm the original. And – it's not for sex – I don't play abject roles and grunt – no, it's quicker going through the customs as a pair. Like getting on the Ark.'

'You'd not leave us?' Tania asks. 'Not just to let Sahrawis realise their wealth?'

'Spread it around, spread it around,' laughs Madame Feng. 'Where there's wealth, there's always need for charitable work. That's a truism.'

'Potash! Madam Feng,' says Francine, teasing. 'That's your game, your aim. Your trickle, your shot. Your goal!'

Football! Teams from all the perilous places, the dangling guys. Anyone could have thought of that! A muster...

Madame Feng ignores her. 'You guys! You take up being gay, and then it's chairs. You're middlebrow, middle, middle,' and she sneers. '"*Langsam, Wozzeck, Langsam*" – sing it with me, relax! The riches have to last a million years, and you'll go through them like a knife, instead! Culture! History! You sit here in your stickiness, no landscapes, no song, no dance. Forgot it all! The best will leave, and leave the rest quite motionless, without a flag, a trophy...'

It should be an invitation – to leave, to prosper. But it seems it's not.

'We did justice,' Tania says. 'That has no price.'

'No guilty one, no prisoner!' shouts Madame Feng. 'No executioner: no one is flung off, down from the minaret, the tower of the winds, no one starves in jail, that pit – spiders and asps, my dears! No judgement. No conscience. Pitiful!'

'The thread's unbroken,' Egon says. 'It mustn't break. That is the lesson, Madame Feng. The law – it must go on, become more complex. But supreme. You can ignore a guy who's maybe guilty, getting off. But it is the law that counts. The universe – its strings: nature – its chain. If these break – we're done for. Chaos. No future: maybe – just flying backwards, over and over, past the "a" in the alphabet, into no tongue, where nothing's spelt, and nothing holds. You look for things you cannot find – but somewhere – they are there. They have to be. You cannot end like Wozzeck, Madame Feng!'

'Maybe Wozzeck was Mister Feng, the first, original,' says Francine, who's middlebrow for sure. 'And Madame Feng changed how it ends.'

Later, Francine says, 'Marcel doesn't make much cash.'

'That's why Madame Feng is moving on,' I say. 'Maybe the RLS is too advanced. She wants the Sahrawis digging for her – but they are all enclosed. To stop her might seem moralistic, though.'

Tania says, 'No one likes Marcel. He is a parasite. The security he gives depends on stronger powers behind. This is a place that flickers, emptying every morning, filling up with guys exhausted. Perhaps you wonder why I stay with him...'

We don't. We are not curious. You have to stay with someone. It's a thing you can't avoid.

Here I am, I came to watch the Tuaregs, learn from their past, their destiny. They're invisible – if they pass, they pass by night – by day, if you're awake and vigilant, in starlight. We can't do anything for them, nor for ourselves. Hugo – his remedies were harsh. You know they have to be. And scattershot. At least, they guarantee a future, if that is what you hope for. Justice, truth too. If those are what you want. Even if they're scattershot.

'This place is perfect, goddam it!' Egon says. 'It aims at no more than it is. No shrugging itself into zoo or landscape, no foodstore, no jewelbox. No gas to pump. Just honesty, all you can see around. And us, a spot of Real Life, quite arbitrary, probably unique.'

'That's why you need a bar,' I say. 'Imagination. That must have a place to stretch and waft. No alcohol, no doors. Just a space, where all the horrors come alive.'

'Transit visas,' Tania says. 'That's what we need, Marcel says. Not given out, but sold. Wholesale them. We sell them to the guys we think are good. Nothing changes – the others, bad guys, will go round. He thinks you'd be good at issuing. The rigorous guys – you'd keep them out. The angry ones – those too you'd bar. You talk about equality, all that – but you're quite a slow methodical. A mollusc on the rock. If you don't do the job, he says, you might not get a visa for yourself. That's his joke, of course! We're the originals here, the friends.'

'It's not a good idea,' I say. 'You'd have to ask the guys who come all sorts of stuff, and search them too. They come on camels or in trucks – they don't want a quiz. A transit visa – it's just that. You pay, you pass. You don't need experts, philosophers, all that.'

'Oh well,' says Tania, shrugging off and looking cold. 'You know how Marcel is. He does some deals that mean we should be clean. Ourselves at least.'

'It would be the end,' I say. 'Real Life would not support it. It would be another bluff. Those – are all around. No one can conquer, no one can resolve. A foreign legion's sent, there's bangs, then silence. We are beyond the limit...'

'Oh stuff!' shouts Francine. 'We always are – that's what exalts us.'

The dodgy guys – pass to the north and south of us. Madame Feng says,

'Stock up my truck – I'm heading West.'

I fill it up with gas. I fill the water cans with gas as well. It will give a sporting chance – how Lia would have loved it! If Madame Feng drives on and out – she'll make it. If not – well, there'll be a lot of thirst. Or even... found, taken for ransom, a rescue with a double face.

I loved dear Madame Feng: she's quite like me. That was her unlucky destiny, to find me, her angel, her lost soul: the traveller lodging in her empty room. I loved poor Alphonse too – and clearly she did not. Sometimes there's retribution.

'I'm a sticky presence,' laughs Madame Feng. 'I hang around when I have gone. My guys, Bosco and Pécuchon, they will represent me. But they won't wear rings. Don't know the hotel business – how you don't use clean sheets, just take the bottom, up to the top, and on and on. Moustache or feet – that's the house aroma, depending on the day.'

'I'm lucky you gave out sheets, Madame Feng,' I say, and she suspects me. Irreverence – a giveaway. You don't laugh about the business, Francine says.

'You got as close as anything to Hugo's state,' says Madame Feng, as if consoling, though she's quite indifferent. 'This here – it's not free trade. Marcel sees to that: you pay! – and no one who can avoid the place would buy or sell. And there's no citizens...'

'No flag!' laughs Tania.

'I doubt it's even to be called "Real Life",' says Madame Feng, revving the motor fiercely.

None of this is near the truth, I think. I hold the red birds tight, like they're a talisman. The little plastic one, the key to my account, draws blood. Hugo will have another chance, I think.

I say to Tania, 'I feel our experience is flawed. I know, experience is everything. But we've ignored a lot. We chose not to see what lay beyond those dunes. Our time here – inconclusive – though we should expect that.'

'Oh no,' she says. 'Of course experience must hold good for everything. You don't want to be called an empirio-critic, surely? Anyway, my character has developed. I handle speed much better too – now there is so little of it. When the end comes, I'll leave Marcel. It's like when I left the future – I want to leave the rhetoric, his protests, the rich laughter of his mates. I dream of an immense sea, of which this must be the enormous shore. I'm so delicate, diving and frolicking – like a squid, or dancing and folding like an octopus – a tiny one, not scary.'

'Yes, Tania, you've neglected dancing. And what of Lia? Will Madame Feng find her, do you think?' I ask.

'I used to be with Lia, now I've the memory. What more can there be?' she asks.

'Lia went East,' I say. 'And Madame Feng goes the other way: of course, they'll maybe circle round, discover one another.'

'I wonder,' says Francine, 'if Lia's character developed. Sure, she had the pace, but all the rest, her narrative...'

'Lia got pissed off,' Tania agrees, 'but if you're stuck, a stone – you're still a noble vision.'

'I'd take on Marcel, if Egon wasn't an obsessive,' Francine sets out her fantasy. 'That's him being a different kind of stone. But maybe I'll just realise my new idea – stamping the faces of the revolutionaries on clothes for all those refugees. That way I'm not dealing in commodities – and possibly the shirts give warmth and hope.'

'No, Francine,' says Tania, 'it's not commodities you'd make, but something else – co-opting ideologies of liberation. That's much worse. It's not necessity. And – you can't use Real Life tools to mix with poor guys' lives – real lives.'

'Is that it, Tania, Francine? Swapping guys and making talk that's quite reactionary?' I ask, 'When we are swept away, we seek, we expect, no monument – but surely, there is loyalty we might maintain?'

'Oh no,' says Tania. 'When I went to school, the first day we were all together in a mass: they said "Forget your miserable beginnings – now, after school, you can do, be anything." So, when it finished, off I went, not to return. They gave me free will, and the universe. Not loyalty. That wasn't bad for one day. That's when I learnt to love the future, hoped to set it out, its paths, its rivers. Maybe the sea it flows to.'

Madame Feng has gone. Her friends have not arrived.

'You were my girl, Tania, before all this,' I say, 'but Lia was my favourite. Singing like a bird...'

'I never heard that,' Tania says. 'I wonder if the birds do sing. They say it's threats, just marking territory and warning off.'

'Singers,' I say, 'they're a jealous species, all of them, all who have two legs.'

Well, we learnt nothing, and we could do nothing different if we had. Madame Feng – she didn't look round at the context either, but she already knew it all.

'Lia and you,' says Tania, 'you weren't gentle with each other.'

'I think that's right,' I say.

It's clear, Madame Feng's hoods have gone elsewhere. Marcel's withdrawn. Ready to make a stand, or make a run. It's all building, building up.

'Listen to me ululate,' says Tania. 'It's something I've learned to do, and do quite well. I'm trying to teach Francine – she can't. Says her tongue's too short.'

'Egon complains of that,' I say.

'They're selling diamond rings down there,' says Tania, pointing down. 'They're cheap. They've got a stack.'

'I'm not proposing an engagement now,' I say. 'I'd need to go off to the bank...'

We hear Francine, making an inadequate bubbling sound.

Justice is being done all round, mostly in silence.

A short guy comes up to us. 'I'm Bosco, Madame Feng engaged me,' so he tells. 'Pécuchon – he missed the bus. He's my strong arm, he'll be here. Meanwhile...'

'Meanwhile,' I say, 'go look for Madame Feng. She's by the bank, she rides a Tuareg. You can't miss.'

'Well,' he says, 'it's true the lady Feng is strange to me. But – maybe I should wait until my pal... These awful noises, beasts in the encampment, things with their throats cut and bleeding out. A mighty ocean here, made up of tiny grains... Security is tight – you've armies all around, militias too, and rule-enforcers, just like us. Though – we weren't engaged for this at all. She said "no danger". We should be soccer referees, though we don't know the rules.'

'Quick!' I shout. 'The rules are Madame Feng's delight. Go! Seek! If you should spot her, all would be explained.'

'She says we should seek out and punish anyone who does her down,' says Bosco. 'I seek. The punishment's the job of Pécuchon.'

'Suppose that Madame Feng was doing bad?' asks Tania.

'Listen,' Bosco says. 'It's not a moral thing. It's not about the quantities, or intuition. Nor of feeling bad, which you might do if you were right, or wrong – quite equally. It's about our rules. One is – not feeling bad. Another is, that where there is a moral quandary – it's irresolvable. The greater good's no good. You have to go with loyalty. Or cash. There is no better guide. I'm sure that's how you work. Unless...' and he smiles, 'unless when you say "that's bad", you refer to rulings quite divine, quite godly, that's not arithmetic, nor best on intuition... In that case – doubt comes in as well. Agnosticism.' Bosco says the word perfectly. He must use it lots. Francine stops her gargling, joins us – Egon too.

'That seems right to me,' says Egon. 'If someone stopped dear Madame Feng from doing wrong by killing her and asking for a ransom – well, everyone does some wrong some way. Even when there's socialism...' and he laughs, and punches my arm muscle, like guys do – 'And everyone deserves the doubt. But, Bosco, if I understand – you are the seeker, Pécuchon is, as it were, the executioner?'

Bosco seems surprised by our calm, our cultivated discourse. 'I thought this was a kind of hell,' he says. 'Just thinking of how hot it gets.'

'No, no,' says Francine. 'Military occupation – that is hell. The discourse is corrupted. Here, it's just a limbo – when bad things occur, it's over quick, and leaves you free to talk. It's occupation: that's what we don't want. For us, the empty room is sign of richness. If you're poor, there's always something in your room. Emptiness is something you attain – you don't, of course, count chairs and carpet, plugs and such.'

'Well,' says Bosco, 'I'm not a furniture guy. And I'm not with the military.'

We don't know what to do with him.

'Pécuchon – he has our envelope,' says Bosco. 'That's the pity. You guys are calm, but some things done round here – you wouldn't do them if you weren't possessed by rage. An anger...!'

'Indifference, perhaps? Conviction?' Francine suggests.

'Yes, that goes in the anger,' Bosco says. 'And you sit here and see it all swirl by. Fear lies upon you all. Don't you feel anger too?'

I look into myself: there's idleness and some indifference. No rage. Maybe after all, I'm humanist.

Bosco talks with Marcel.

'They always say there's more that's coming up behind,' says Tania. 'Those military guys! Pécuchon – a made-up name... Soldiers! They take the cash for legions when there's only one or two of them...'

'Well,' I say, 'Beau Geste's a made-up name as well. It didn't help the business here.'

'You don't grasp it,' Tania says. 'Things change. Decisively. Maybe we should go down South, sit there like Hugo, watch it turn around.'

The thought's alarming. Real Life is maybe coming to its end. Everywhere is full of people, impossible to turn around. Especially, down South.

Bosco says, 'Militia or army – it's the same. You need a mission. Lay or godly. It's a glue. Call it the constitution, call it the Plan, the Rule. The guys need something to make them stick. Then, it's arms. The better they are, the swifter they resolve. Otherwise, it's prophecies, machetes, and the corps à corps.'

'That's Marcel's plan?' I ask. 'A militia? Tania didn't say.'

'Oh,' says Bosco, 'she creeps into his cot, when the thought occurs. But she's renounced her mission.'

'You're such a cynic, Bosco,' Francine laughs, 'That's what I like about Egon, he's just lost his illusions. He doesn't make it a philosophy.'

The time for me to take control is near – perhaps it's just gone by. At any rate, the time is right, or round about.

Marcel calls us all. 'Full house!' he shouts. 'At least three jokers here, their mouths agape! A wonder pack.'

'A dance!' says Francine, spinning round.

'Yes,' says Marcel, 'but only Tania is involved. A rite we shall remember. Bosco has settled things – with our security. Not just from guys marauding – but keeping safe our territory. We don't need our flag. We do need our future guaranteed. A mission. Safe in our city here, without the walls. He'll look for those who've disappeared – somewhere they'll have agglomerated...'

We don't follow him. 'You signed my secrets act,' he says, 'so you must know it all. The story, the design.'

Marcel passes me a bottle – green liquid, must be Lia's absinthe – but no! It's water.

'Just algae,' Marcel says. 'It's better for you, fertile.'

We think of Clara, swimming in the fertile river, being boarded by snails.

'The dance before the throne – come on Tania!' Marcel says.

'I'll be that bear,' says Tania. Marcel puts on the mask, the barman's face, the weathered skin. There is no body – only his own. Tania's the bear. She puts a ram's horn behind each ear, two staves to keep her upright. And a scaly tail. A bear from dreams. Francine lights up her spliff, her red brown yellow face is shiny as a cherry. Egon's sideburns in the blue light seem tattoos.

Tania dances, her brown hair stops just above the nipples, as she goes rocking to and fro, the giant staves keep her upright, slow her down. She staggers: yes – those small features – they could be a bear's, the pinkish nose, the teddy's eyes. She's in distress. Maybe she thinks of those who disappeared, or those who are not there but have a tomb, a record, a glyph, a hole.

'Bravo, Tania,' Bosco shouts. 'When we have recruited lads, you'll lead the entertainment on!'

'No, no,' says Marcel, mumbling from behind his mask. 'This is not the message, not the show we need.

True, I do my penance but – Tania ought to jazz things up...'

She keeps her rhythm, her yellow eyes pan round us all, constant and special.

'Look!' shouts Marcel. 'Where is the relevance? A dance of fire, of spring, of ecstasy – not this tired lumbering...'

Tania carries on. It is her art. You do not interrupt.

Francine – to calm Marcel, maybe to ingratiate herself, to change the music – puts her arms around Marcel, the chief. Bosco makes a sound – a fart, a belch – derision is beneath it all, though there's no words.

Egon objects. We hadn't thought he cared. 'Come on, Francine,' he says, quite menacing, and 'Fuck off, Marcel,' he concludes. 'End this charade. You have no power, Marcel, no lesson – just cash to buy some marginals who'll do atrocious things with or without your ordering...'

His is the tone that closes bars, that sobers everyone. Incites.

'Egon! Enough,' says Marcel. 'That is enough.'

'The fault is Tania's,' Egon says, stirring things up, or mediating.

'She has no fault,' says Marcel, taking off the face-mask, 'If there is fault, it is Francine. Sets herself to be a judge, but she's betrayed the ideals of Real Life State. Selling those rocks, she makes a mockery of our philosophy...'

'A rockery, she's made,' laughs Bosco. Marcel and Egon don't react to him, they spar up to each other.

'No, no, this is impossible,' shouts Tania, waving both her staves. 'Think of the example, all the interpretations, squabbles over women, masks, the dance

... this is not at all why we are here,' and every word incites Marcel, Egon. Philosophy arises in each brain. Why are we here, what have we done, will do? Where are the absent ones, who'll look for them, who will attack, who take over the Beau Geste?

'We have a mission here,' shouts Marcel. 'Cost what it may...'

'Cheap *condottieri* that's all you are,' Egon shouts back. 'Destroyer of our guiding stars: dear Lia – Madame Feng as well, for all that she was scum.'

Bosco looks anxious, but generally, he laughs.

Francine jumps in: 'Hey, guys, we mustn't fight. Each sings their song, dances their dance, and then it's done, it's finished, on there comes another turn. The past exists to be forgot.'

We all stare angrily at her.

'I have no turn,' I say. 'Francine – from you, no song, no dance. I wait my opportunity to go down South, turn things around...'

'Then go!' Marcel shouts at me. 'Here, nothing turns around. We spin, we gyre, and sing and dance – we keep our patch, our tiny spot of paradise, decent and clean – it does not change, we shall defend...'

'Oh yes,' says Bosco. 'That's for me. We'll build some walls and bunkers here...'

'No, no,' says Egon. 'This place – it's a refuge. Entertainment, proper rooms, with furniture, bars for dreams and roistering...'

We're all angry now.

'Militias truncate the Real Life,' Egon shouts.

Tania dances on, gripping her staves.

'We've done some awful things, Marcel, us two, but this is quite the worst,' Egon says, pretending to calm himself.

'Aha!' says Marcel, 'you mean the women haven't done as bad? That's stereotype. The beautiful go free, they're innocent until the executioner calls, at most the women are accomplices. There's the myth, the tale! We, men, do; they stay home and clean the hut!'

'No, not at all,' says Francine, anxious to confess some crime.

'I'm not a beauty,' Tania grunts. 'And I don't want a punishment.'

'It's all about the genres,' says Bosco mildly, knowing this annoys. 'Defence is part of the attack. You must prepare for both. This here's a haven, but some guys can ride right in, do what they wish...'

'There's nothing here to wish!' says Marcel, furious. 'Enrol those guys and give them guns. We are the only objects of desire, Tania and myself. Now Lia's gone, and Madame Feng, the jewels, the champions, are no more. We are the rags that once held bright flesh, ambitions – now, we are just sets of bones that lions have gnawed.'

'Not yet, Marcel,' laughs Bosco. 'I'm here protecting what is left. And if they kill you – I have marked out plots. In those deep tombs, the animals won't delve. You'll be anonymous and undisturbed, while we'll march on and sing our songs...' He struts a little. Maybe he thinks of conquest, maybe of a personal tomb, like Clara's, not built of clay, but of obsidian, with razor wire on top.

I hope this talk of singing may awake my lovely birds. The tiny plastic one – that is my key, my safeguard, my best friend. I grasp it tight.

Marcel stands, throws down the mask. 'Egon, Tania, and the useless one,' and he points at me. 'Fuck off. Francine will stay and make commodities – a compromise, quite temporary. Bosco will do his work. The rest – away, away! Join with the disappeared!'

It's a Greek moment. We hold our poses, stand like marbles. Eternal, for a moment, dumbed by edict. Marcel shouts, 'And take the bear!'

Tania grunts.

'I'll start all over,' Egon says. 'Back to the Empty Room. New York is full of mangroves now – the sea! the sea! Here it is, it marches in – the monkeys eat their pawpaws where the brokers used to boast and frolic... Smell the spices, see the flying fish that sail up Broadway – maybe there are dolphins too – and Indians! The Nations, all Six, once more united! It will all be theirs again, a federation of the dispossessed... see their war canoes, driving along Wall Street... And me! Above them all, presiding in my bar, pouring from dawn to sunset; shamans' drums – yes, we'll have a group of prophesiers, on contract... who would have thought, when we were into future games, that this would come about, would be the unforeseen?' And on he talks, the vision and the tongues are on him, irresistible.

'Yes!' says Tania. 'Every forecaster would love a revelation bright and rounded like that one. The match decisive, better than football, whatever are its rules. Back will come the sea, the tropics, and the Nations! How could we have missed all that, our models – rooted in our property, our dreams of riches, problems solved... all fantasies and wishful thoughts...! Fly, Egon, fly – take up your future, away from this pale fake, real life that's coming to an end...'

I'm not that interested – now it's my time, and my decision. 'We won't go back,' I say. 'Tania, we're going South. I'll get the cash, and you – revert to human speech! Throw down your staves. We'll find a pickup that is heading East, then take a road, a train, head down to Hugo's land...'

Tania – she's still under some influence – and I, we, gaze over Real Life State. Clara's mausoleum has lost a wall, the beams that held the roof are quite askew. 'Empty tombs, and empty wombs,' sings Tania. 'Add up to empty rooms. So what? It's broken, totally, now she can escape, seek out her son. So what? – another ruin – there's ruins all around, and maps of what has disappeared. And a machine, that looks beneath the sand, and picks out what is not and what has never been.'

'Yes, Tania,' I say, pushing away the lumbering furry thing she has become. 'We'll go down South. I have my bird, my key, my guarantee, our cash. I need two names – one, for the bank. One for the account. A map, to find them both. I have to think, reflect. Memory returns, it's like a dictionary. It's mostly stuff irrelevant, you mustn't linger or you forget what you were looking for. You need to know an alphabet, not be led astray by curiosities...'

'That's not how I work at all,' says Tania, livening up. 'If you go on like that, your language will be random.'

'I just forget,' I say. 'Give me some names. and maybe when we find the place, we'll find our Lia too. She's sure to wait...'

'Oh no,' says Tania. 'Not Lia. It is true I loved – but if we find her – only one of us can go with her, ride on her Tuareg. The other, abandoned – you'd be cooked...'

We find her bike. No sign of her – and where's the bank? There's *Les choses de la vie*, the hardware store.

No line of banks, no timbers even. Flown away. Maybe it's the wrong place.

'There's her Tuareg,' Tania says. 'Maybe it's a sign. The Tuaregs have an empire, one of those almost invisible, like the Yueh Chi, until they settled down. Maybe theirs is the new, the destiny.'

Someone should recognise my plastic bird. Where? Who?

'Those characters we left behind,' says Tania. 'To us they seem prosaic – really, they're exceptional. Firm in adversity, and full of plans. Egon, Marcel, Francine! Oh, how I miss them – even more than those who disappeared.'

We'll have to walk, an epic march. Tania – sometimes she is still the bear. 'Maybe I shan't fit in,' she says, and I reply, 'You should have thought of that before...'

We trek on down – like the Bantu, like Afrikaners in their ox-carts... into forests full of riches. In the capital there's God the Father, helping guys cut down the precious trees, just like another God made cash out of his Eden, speculating in the animals, and tweaking them.

'This is French Congo, not the Belgian one,' I say. 'It must be rationalist, and quite humane,' but Tania grunts. We're lost for months, as round and round we go, stumbling in mineshafts, dodging the pythons drooping from the glorious trees, their diamond eyes interrogating...

Here's some charcoal-burners. 'They will give us eat,' I say. But no, the chief guy talks of some religious stuff – 'Jesus is Afrodite, syncretising love and war,' he says. 'When we went on our trek from South to North, the mother of us all took root in northern Syria – goddess of love, no less... and all the seers and wizards that have followed her – made sense of love and war, the conquest and the settlement... And where do you fit in?' he asks. 'There's no bears here. No Left or Right, just hanging on and hanging in, some alcohol, some prayers...'

'It's all right, Tania,' I say. 'We're on an epic march. It's right we meet with guys who stereotype,' but we are weary now. We cross the rivers and the tracks, the deserts and the grassy plains.

At last, the demons in our path defeated quite conclusively, we see poor Hugo's shack. There is no roof, of course.

'Where shall we sleep?' asks Tania. Offhand, I say, 'Bears sleep on the floor.' She weeps.

I put my three birds in the empty cage. I put the folded Real Life flag to cover them. It's home. This is at last an empty room. Here, I can start to turn things round.

How Tania talks! ... of all the ones who've disappeared, or those we've left behind. The Beau Geste... I find a tiny radio, and turn it up to keep her quiet. It's playing *Ariadne auf Naxos.*

'There, Tania,' I say. 'Maybe it was all about you from the start. You gave the thread that led us from the labyrinth, and then you ended bad. That is the way it goes.'

'I'm not so sure,' she says. 'I didn't lead you anywhere. I talk and talk, your goddam birds don't sing, or open up accounts. We're poor as poor, like all the others here. Hugo at least had his pretensions, we have none.'

'No, Tania, you're quite wrong,' I say. 'We were misled before. This is real life, not what we left behind.'

The empty tomb – exactly as it was when I was here and Hugo'd died. No animals in sight, no tourists snapping them.

'A little tenderness at least,' says Tania, crumbling.

'There's no elephants in sight,' I say, trying to rouse her. 'None we can exploit. We've come through an Eden – French Congo, though. Madame Feng's brooch, her ivory, came from the Belgian side.'

'Those trees!' says Tania. 'Not a fruit upon them. The snakes quite wordless, drooping down.'

'The apples are imported,' I say. 'Gooseberries from China, too, no doubt.'

The opera winds on... 'See!' I say. 'It's not a distant corpse awaits, not your dead lover's sail, on the horizon speeding here. Cheer up, Tania. It's Bacchus!'

And here's a jug of homebrew: 'The neighbours gave,' I say. 'Good folk. They won the football. Now, listen to the record! Bacchus! Rejoice!' They sing, the opera concludes.

'Oh,' says Tania, much cheered. 'You're too labyrinthine for me! You're happy. You've found the empty room here – no body, no song, no roof. There must be more, for you. For me, there's nothing. After my sacrifice...'

We drink. It's powerful hooch. She's happy now.

'Look up, Tania, look up,' I say. 'Forget projections, forget eating them – forget Lia, and Marcel. Look at the stars, their pattern. Forget your hunger and your poverty. It's not at all about the people being poor. Tomorrow, we'll start to turn the things around.'

*

She listens to me, trying to convince herself, and I go on,

'In a while, you'll hear the singing start again, and the music for your dance.'

About the author

John Fraser has lived in Rome since 1980. Previously, he worked in England and Canada.